THE KISS OF LIFE

Just for you, straight from the pen of the world's most famous romantic novelist.

Ajax Audenshaw is the one man who can help archaeologist Lord Yelverton find a long-lost treasure trove. Although wary and resentful, Tula, Audenshaw's beautiful daughter, agrees to guide Yelverton through the Mexican jungle to find the hidden cave of a past civilisation. Strange powers overcome them both as what begins as a search for priceless objects becomes a quest for the mysterious forces of Quetzalcoatl, god of rain and the morning star...

THE KISS OF LIFE

The Kiss Of Life

by
Barbara Cartland

Magna Large Print Books
Long Preston, North Yorkshire,
England.

British Library Cataloguing in Publication Data.

Cartland, Barbara
    The kiss of life.

A catalogue record for this book is
available from the British Library

ISBN 0-7505-1110-9

First published in Great Britain by Hutchinson, 1981

Copyright © 1981 by Barbara Cartland

Cover illustration by arrangement with Rupert Crew Ltd.

The moral right of the author has been asserted

Published in Large Print 1998 by arrangement with Rupert
Crew Ltd.

Magna Large Print is an imprint of
Library Magna Books Ltd.
Printed and bound in Great Britain by
T.J. International Ltd., Cornwall, PL28 8RW.

AUTHOR'S NOTE

I visited Mexico first in 1967 and again in 1980 and found it a fascinating country, full of mystery. Its suffering under the Spaniards and the brutality they inflicted on the Mexican-Indians did not quench a faith which still survives.

Mexico is full of gods and magics, demons and witches and a beauty that catches your heart.

As I have described in this novel, marvellous treasures of the past have been found already but there are many more to be unearthed and reclaimed from the jungle.

In 1930 golden treasure fashioned by the Mixtecs was taken from one tomb at Monte Albán. In another, the Ruler had been buried with objects of amber, coral, rock crystal and carved jaguar bones.

Modern Mexicans have outwardly accepted Christianity but even Mexican Catholicism is a unique blend of two cultures and the native religions remain.

Birds are sacrificed and the fields sprinkled with their blood to ensure a good crop. The Huichol Indians sacrifice an ox as part of their rain ceremonies.

Pregnant women all over Mexico carry something made of iron under their belts to ward off the ill effects of an eclipse of the moon on their unborn children.

Women who look like witches sell baskets of herbs near the Cathedral in Mexico City and I was offered one, which I was warned was L.S.D.

I love Mexico, the one universal disadvantage is that everyone sooner or later seems to get Montezuma's revenge which is an upset tummy.

But the sky is blue, the hills green, the flowers brilliant, the sun shines, and it is

so beautiful you hold your breath in case
it is a mirage.

Who could ask for anything nearer
Heaven?

1

Riding on the best horse obtainable Lord Yelverton knew that he had a long journey ahead of him.

A railway line ran from Mexico City as far as Iguala, but from there the journey had to be made on horseback to Acapulco where he had what for him was an appointment of considerable importance.

He had always known that things in Mexico would be primitive, with an amazing contrast between the upper classes, the Creoles and Mestizos, and the poor, downtrodden Indians whose conditions grew worse year by year.

What he had not expected was that the country would be so beautiful.

There were mountains in the far distance, their peaks silhouetted against the sky dazzling with snow, trees covered the nearby hills, streams twisting low in the valley were silver with an occasional cascade breaking in a roaring torrent down into a pool.

Here there were the mauve heads of the *lirio,* the water hyacinth and beneath the trees and along the path over which Lord Yelverton was riding there were flowers vivid in every colour, besides the strange, almost ghoulish shapes of the cactus, one or two of them in flower.

The whole country seemed to have an agelessness about it which made Lord Yelverton feel that he rode into eternity and there was no point in hurrying.

He knew this was the lassitude which affected all Mexicans, especially when they were on the high plateau where Mexico City now stood on the site of many cities before it.

He had been studying the history of the magnificent and mighty Indian Empires which went back thousands of years and which would doubtless rise again for as many in the future.

He was, in fact, intent on discovering for himself some of the treasures of the people who had practised soldering and filigree plating as early as A.D. 1000.

The story of these treasures had excited him until he knew he would never rest until he had visited Mexico to find, if he could, some of them for himself.

An archaeologist for some years, his name was already known in Egypt among the tombs of the Kings, and in Turkey where he had unearthed many ancient sites that had not been known before.

The Roman remains in Libya owed much to his enthusiasm and the money he contributed to their discovery.

He had always thought that Mexico would be his El Dorado, but he had meant to wait a little while after an expedition to Egypt. Then strange circumstances had brought him here sooner than he expected.

Everyone in Mexico City had wanted to

talk to him of Mexico's future, but Lord Yelverton was intent on his own business and had no intention of being involved in other people's politics.

He was a man of not yet thirty-two and he had a controlled reserve which made him seem aloof and an authority which those who served him found intimidating.

They would in fact, have been surprised if they had known that there was an irrepressible feeling of excitement in his breast as he led the way followed by a motley collection of horses and mules carrying his luggage and servants who had volunteered eagerly to escort him to Acapulco.

He was glad to be away from the Capital with its crowds of pale-faced Mexicans, politicians, professional and business people, all calculating, Lord Yelverton thought, how they could exploit his visit in one way or another.

The hospitality and comfort he had found there had not enticed him to stay, and he preferred the open country that he had seen from the railway train and even the infinite dryness unmitigated by the fields of wheat and maize and the more brilliant fields of bright-green sugar-cane.

Outside the city the Mexican man walked in a different way, jauntily balancing his huge hat, with thrown-back shoulders and a folded *serape* like a Royal mantle.

Lord Yelverton noticed that most of them were handsome with dark skin and black hair which gleamed like rich feathers.

The Indians might have a feeling of hopelessness but they were unbroken, determined and resilient, even laughing with indifferent carelessness at a future which appeared almost as grim as the past.

And yet in Mexico, more than anywhere else in the world, Lord Yelverton knew the past was indivisible from the future.

He was certain that if he had discovered treasures and antiquities in other lands, there was a great deal more to be discovered in Mexico than anywhere else.

The Pyramids were already occupying the attention and learning of archaeologists, Temples and shrines were being excavated, and Museums all over the civilized world were competing with each other for the carvings, vases and pottery that were being unearthed.

Lord Yelverton however, was not interested in what concerned other enthusiasts of past cultures, but in something that he kept secret to himself and had in fact, mentioned to only one man since he had arrived in Mexico.

When he had been travelling back from Egypt, a seaman aboard the ship had approached him and showed him a small carved jaguar bone which he said he carried for luck.

Lord Yelverton realized that the mythical scene depicted on it was of a very early culture and he had asked the man where it had come from.

'I'm a Mexican, M'Lord.'

'You found this on one of the sites that was being excavated?' Lord Yelverton enquired.

The man shook his head. Then he asked eagerly:

'It's valuable? You'll give me money for it?'

Lord Yelverton had already sized up the Mexican, seen the greed in his black eyes, and noted the sudden smile that seemed to transform his usually sullen expression.

'I will certainly buy it from you,' he said, and named a sum which made the seaman gasp.

He deliberately gave the man more than he expected, and as he had anticipated, he soon produced from his pocket another small object.

It was of amber, the deep rich amber that had almost been lost to the Western World, and that too was carved.

Lord Yelverton knew then that he had

in his hands two almost perfect treasures of antiquity that had lasted all the centuries of disruption, destruction and warfare.

He was not surprised when on reaching Mexico he approached the greatest expert he could consult to learn that what he now possessed had doubtless come from the classical period of Monte Albán.

'There must still be a great deal to be unearthed in that region,' the Curator had said. 'There is an expedition setting out next month to search for tombs, and I expect sensational results from their findings.'

Lord Yelverton knew that the Rulers of the Mixtecs who had brought most of the Zapotec territory under their sway had been buried with finely worked objects of gold, silver, amber, jet and coral, and necklaces of rock crystal.

He had also heard stories of thousands of pearls ranging in size up to that of a pigeon's egg.

He had no intention of visiting Monte

Albán which he was certain was already overrun by eager archaeologists, but planned to go instead due south of Mexico City to Acapulco.

When the seaman had first mentioned it, it was only a name to Lord Yelverton, until his research on returning to England showed him that the Spaniards led by Cortez had reached Acapulco in about 1530.

The ships from this port sailed to the other jewel in Spain's new Empire, Peru, and from there they had even explored the Gulf of California.

After they had seized Mexico and most of central and southern America, the Spaniards were determined to conquer the Philippines.

Lord Yelverton's history books told him that the first Spanish vessels sailed East from Manila in 1565, across the Pacific and eventually arrived in Acapulco, opening one of the world's most important trading-posts.

Ships from China and Japan regularly arrived there from which their cargos were loaded on mules to be carried across to Veracruz on the Atlantic coast, and from there to be shipped to Spain.

When the Spaniards left, with them went the trade to the Far East and Acapulco declined into what it had been before, a small, unimportant fishing-village.

It was a place that Lord Yelverton would not have thought of visiting had not one man whom he had been advised to trust in Mexico City told him that was where he must go.

'Why?' Lord Yelverton enquired.

'Because, My Lord, you have to meet Ajax Audenshaw.'

'Who is he?'

The Curator looked surprised.

'You must have heard of him, My Lord. His reports to the Geographical Society are sensational, and his book published four years ago about the Aztecs revealed more about their civilization than all research

20

had hitherto achieved.'

'But of course,' Lord Yelverton conceded. 'Now I know who you mean!'

'He is a strange man and always unpredictable,' the Curator said, ruminatively, 'but he is, in fact, the only person who can help you in that particular neighbourhood, and without his guidance your journey would be completely fruitless.'

This was plain speaking and Lord Yelverton looked surprised, but the Curator went on:

'I am quite certain the people would resent a foreigner interfering with their dead, however many thousands of years ago they died.'

There was a twist to Lord Yelverton's lips as he asked:

'Are you suggesting in a somewhat roundabout way that it might be dangerous for me to search for the cave without Audenshaw's protection?'

The Curator smiled.

'That, My Lord, is exactly what I am

trying to convey to you, and feeling a little embarrassed in doing so.'

'Then of course I must accept your advice,' Lord Yelverton conceded, 'and call on Mr Audenshaw.'

Again the Curator smiled.

'Let me warn you he will not be what you expect. In fact I understand at the moment he has ceased his research into Ancient Civilizations and has taken up painting.'

'Painting?' Lord Yelverton exclaimed. 'Surely that is a waste of his great knowledge and experience in other fields?'

'I believe quite a number of distinguished people have tried to persuade Audenshaw that he is wasting his time,' the Curator said, 'but he is a law unto himself. If he wishes to paint, he will paint. And what is more, My Lord, if he will not assist you there will be nothing you can do about it but go home!'

Lord Yelverton was so surprised that he could not, for the moment, reply and the

Curator said tentatively:

'If that happens—though let us hope for Your Lordship's sake it will not—I would of course be very grateful of the opportunity to purchase the two objects you have shown me, especially the jaguar bone which is better than anything I have seen so far.'

'They are not for sale,' Lord Yelverton said coldly.

He thanked the Curator for his help, took a last perfunctory look at Mexico City and set off for Acapulco, grateful that he could at least travel some of the way by train.

Five days later Lord Yelverton found himself within sight of his objective.

The weather had grown much warmer, in fact in the middle of the day it was so hot that both he and his entourage found it easier to rest in the shadow of the trees, then proceed late in the afternoon when it grew cooler.

Yet there was always the breeze from

the sea, and even sometimes a cool wind blowing from the distant mountains which kept Lord Yelverton invigorated and not as mentally tired as he had half-expected he might be.

He had also grown increasingly curious about the man he had to seek out on arrival.

They had stayed on the way, not in Inns since none existed, but in small villages, sleeping in the tent that he had been wise enough to bring with him and talking with the local inhabitants.

Sometimes this was outside the only place where one could purchase a drink, at others on the steps of the inevitable huge half-ruined Church, its barrel roof crouching like an animal, its domes glittering with yellow or blue tiles, many of them broken or riddled with shot.

Lord Yelverton would watch the quiet native women in long skirts moving on the roofs as they hung out their washing, or spreading it on the hot stones.

24

There was invariably an old Priest with whom he could converse in Spanish or sometimes the manager of a hacienda had come into the village in search of companionship after a hard day's work in the fields.

Everyone he talked to was intensely curious as to where he was going, and when he told them it was to meet Ajax Audenshaw they nodded their heads as if it was what they expected, since there could be no other reason for anyone to go to Acapulco.

It was through the Priests that Lord Yelverton gathered that Audenshaw's way of living was a scandal, but what he had not expected was to learn that he was English.

He had thought because of his name that he would be Scandinavian.

'No, *Señor,*' a Priest told him. '*Señor* Audenshaw is English, but with I think, a Swedish ancestor, who accounts for his fair hair.'

'You have met him?' Lord Yelverton asked.

The Priest nodded.

'He stops here as the *Señor* is doing, if he is going to Mexico or perhaps to Taxco when he is in need of gaiety or a new woman.'

Lord Yelverton looked surprised at his last words, and the Priest laughed at the expression on his face.

'When, *Señor*, you meet the Englishman you will understand. He is like your pirates who pillaged Spanish ships when they sailed from Acapulco in the old days, but *Señor* Audenshaw pillages women.'

'Women?' Lord Yelverton questioned.

The Priest put up his hands in an expressive gesture of disapproval.

'He is a buccaneer, *Señor*, and no woman can resist him.'

The same words were repeated several times and Lord Yelverton thought it was not at all the sort of person he had envisaged writing a scholarly book on the

Aztec civilization or being respected for his knowledge by the Curator in Mexico City.

'They must be mistaken,' he told himself. 'That sort of behaviour does not sound English.'

At the last place they stopped for the night he had been told exactly where Audenshaw's house was to be found.

Now he saw the port of Acapulco ahead of him, and came down out of the green hills to feel almost blinded by the sparkling blue of the sea bordered by the golden sand of the beaches.

The flowers had increased in profusion and there was colour everywhere, especially the crimson and yellow of the hibiscus trees with their large blossoms that seemed almost over-poweringly luxuriant.

In fact the colour everywhere seemed to be in almost a crude contrast to the poverty-stricken appearance of the men and women moving along the dusty roads.

Yet everything Lord Yelverton saw was

beautiful, more beautiful than he had anticipated, and he searched as he had been told to do for the sheep-track that would lead him to the bay that Audenshaw had made his own.

As he did so, he quickened the pace of his horse because he was eager to see the man about whom he had heard so much.

Audenshaw's long, low house built in Spanish fashion was party dilapidated and yet at the same time was, Lord Yelverton told himself, what he might have expected.

There were creepers growing over the broken walls, young goats, chickens and pigs wandering about unattended, while small cardinal birds with scarlet bodies and brilliant purple heads flashed among the thick green leaves of the trees.

As he neared the house his grey eyes missing nothing, Lord Yelverton thought it was an unusual place for an Englishman to live, especially one with the talents and achievements of Audenshaw.

He reached the dry sand, well trodden in front of the house and a boy appeared from somewhere to stare at him in surprise. Then as if remembering his instructions he came towards him to take the bridle of his horse.

'I wish to speak to *Señor* Audenshaw,' Lord Yelverton said in Spanish.

In answer the boy jerked his thumb towards the house and dismounting Lord Yelverton walked up several broken stone steps and onto the verandah.

He was conscious, now that he had arrived, that he was tired and a little stiff. He also felt extremely thirsty and hoped that at least he would be offered something to drink.

As there appeared to be no-one about he walked from the verandah into a large, untidy room.

There were things scattered everywhere, shawls, baskets, children's toys, but the chairs and sofas looked comfortable and there were Lord Yelverton noticed, vases of flowers in English fashion, on several of the tables.

The place seemed strangely quiet.

There was a staircase at the far end of the room, and since the house seemed to extend further, he walked on.

Then for the first time he heard a sound. It was someone humming and it seemed in such an atmosphere, strangely inappropriate that it should be *The British Grenadiers*.

There was a doorway without a door and he walked through it and found himself in a Studio.

It was not in the least like any Studio he had ever seen before, but because there were some canvasses lying about on the floor and on easels, it was obvious what it was.

There were windows opening on to yet another verandah and at the far end of the room, half hidden from view by an easel holding a large, unfinished canvas, he saw to his astonishment a naked woman.

She was a negress, young with an exquisitely curved slim body that looked like polished ebony.

She was standing with her head tipped back, her arm raised as if on the point of drinking from a crystal goblet that glittered in the light.

Then as he stared at her Lord Yelverton was aware that she was posing for a man who was seated on a low stool and bending towards his canvas.

Lord Yelverton moved a little closer and there was no doubt from the fair head he could see outlined against the blazing colour with which he was painting, that this was Audenshaw.

He walked forward to introduce himself, when as he stopped, the painter asked sharply in English:

'Who the devil are you?'

'Forgive my intrusion,' Lord Yelverton said, 'but I could find no-one at the door, so I entered the house.'

As he spoke the man to whom he was

31

speaking turned round and looked at his visitor.

Then Lord Yelverton saw that the descriptions he had heard were not exaggerated.

In his early forties Ajax Audenshaw was still an extremely handsome and unusual-looking man.

His hair, as the Priest had said, was so thick and fair that he had obviously inherited it from some Swedish ancestor, but his features were very English, and his blue eyes seemed to add a touch of colour to his skin burnt brown by the sun.

For a moment the two men stared at each other. Then Ajax Audenshaw rose to his feet.

Lord Yelverton was over six foot tall but the older man topped him by at least three inches and with his broad shoulders he looked like a Viking.

Lord Yelverton held out his hand.

'My name is Yelverton,' he said, 'and I

have come here from Mexico City because I am told you are the only man who can help me.'

As he spoke he was aware that Ajax Audenshaw was staring at him searchingly, almost as if he was weighing him up and deciding in his own mind whether he was worth knowing, or if he should turn him from the door.

Then he smiled and it made him look younger and more friendly.

'Nice to hear an English voice,' he said. 'Will you have a drink?'

'It is something I have been looking forward to,' Lord Yelverton replied.

As if he suddenly remembered his model, Ajax Audenshaw said in Spanish:

'That'll be all, Carlotta. You can go now. Come again tomorrow.'

The naked girl put down the crystal goblet, which Lord Yelverton noted was an extremely fine one, and spoke in Mexican-Spanish, which was difficult to understand.

Ajax Audenshaw obviously knew what

she wanted and taking a small coin from his pocket he tossed it across the room to her.

She caught it deftly, looked at it disparagingly, shrugged her shoulders, picked up her clothes from the chair adjacent to where she had been standing and dressing without the least embarrassment, walked while she was still half-naked onto the verandah to disappear into the garden.

Audenshaw paid no attention to her but went to the other door.

'Ramon! Miquel!' he shouted. 'Bring some beer and mind it's cold or I'll skin you both alive!'

Far away in the interior of the house there was a chorus of: *Si, si, Señor!'* and Audenshaw walked back towards Lord Yelverton to say:

'Those damned servants are always sleeping. If you can get more than an hour's work out of anyone in this place you are lucky.'

'It is too beautiful for people to do

anything but look around them,' Lord Yelverton remarked, surprised at his lyrical outburst which was unlike his usual way of speaking.

'Beautiful,' Audenshaw agreed, 'and almost impossible to convey on canvas.'

He glanced at one or two of the pictures lying about and as Lord Yelverton followed the direction of his eyes he realized that it was the flowers, the sea, the mountains and the natives that Ajax Audenshaw was trying to capture in a very strange way.

He had heard of the Impressionists and had never been particularly enamoured of their work, but because he had spent a great deal of time in France he understood a little of what they were trying to convey by the way they depicted light.

He saw that Audenshaw was using the same technique on the fantastic, violent colours of Mexico, and the effect was not only sensational, but had, he thought, almost the result of being over-emotional to those who looked at it.

Audenshaw had, he thought, a strange, savage, almost primitive talent that could be found only in a man who felt deeply and was influenced by the exotic mixture of strange civilizations and even stranger people he painted.

He walked from one canvas to another while Audenshaw watched him with an amused smile on his face. Then he said:

'Come on! Be honest! You don't like what I have done and you think I am wasting my time!'

'I have not said so,' Lord Yelverton expostulated.

'But you are English! How could you think anything else?'

'I do not think it is a question of criticizing but of understanding what you are trying to convey.'

He saw that Audenshaw was impressed by his reply.

Then the beer arrived, the cool, light, delicious Mexican beer which Lord Yelverton had already discovered was different from what he had drunk anywhere else in the world.

He accepted a glass of it gratefully.

They moved out onto the verandah where it was cooler and sat in chairs which were comfortable, but in need of having their seats and backs repaired.

It was then Lord Yelverton realized how unconventionally his host was dressed, wearing the loose white calico drawers of the Mexican peasant which flopped around his ankles as he walked, while on the rest of his body there appeared to be only a sleeveless white vest splashed and stained from the paints he had been using.

Yet because of Audenshaw's height he looked as magnificent as if he was wearing the armour in which the Spaniards had conquered the country or the great plumed golden headdress of the Aztecs.

They drank a little while in silence. Then Audenshaw said:

'You had better tell me what I can do for you. I cannot believe you want to buy one of my paintings.'

He was mocking himself and Lord Yelverton replied:

'I might well do that before I leave, but actually I came on a different mission.'

'I should have thought you had enough to do in Egypt without coming to Mexico!'

Lord Yelverton was surprised.

'You know who I am?'

'I heard there was a stranger riding in this direction three days ago and when I was told he was a foreigner, I suspected he would be coming to see me.'

'I am still flattered that you should have heard of my work in Egypt,' Lord Yelverton said, 'but I suppose even in Acapulco the Geographical reports arrive sooner or later.'

'Usually later,' Audenshaw replied. 'It is a pity that last tomb had been rifled before you opened it.'

'It was heart-breaking,' Lord Yelverton admitted.

'Here the robbers have not been so busy

but they are now arriving in well financed expeditions, with permits to dig, and in a few years Mexico will be barren and deprived of her memories of the past.'

'I think it will take perhaps a few hundred years.'

'I hope you are right,' Audenshaw replied. 'But when whatever they find has been placed in Museums, the tombs and temples will be no more than Mausoleums. I prefer them to remain protected by the jungle growing over them so that they are almost impossible to locate.'

Lord Yelverton sighed.

'You are depressing me,' he said, 'when I have come here to show you these.'

He took the jaguar bone and the amber carving as he spoke, from his pocket and held them out.

Ajax Audenshaw stared at them as they lay in the palm of his hand and then took them from him.

He held them with fingers that Lord

Yelverton realized despite his size were gentle and sensitive. Then he said:

'They are undoubtedly from Monte Albán, and no-one but the Mixtecs are capable of such artistry.'

'That is what I understood,' Lord Yelverton replied, 'and as a matter of fact they came from near here.'

'That is impossible!'

'Not according to the story I was told.'

'Tell me!'

'I bought these from a Mexican seaman who was working as one of the crew of the ship in which I returned from Egypt to England. He wanted some money to go ashore at Gibraltar and I bought them from him for far more than he had expected.'

'Why did you give him so much?'

'Because I wanted to know from where he had obtained them.'

'Did he tell you?'

'The story was, and he made it sound very convincing, that a Spaniard who had access to one of the Mixtec tombs had obtained by devious means, a great number of precious objects for himself without declaring them to any of his fellow Spaniards. He was a man of substance, and he decided to take them back to Spain with him and arranged to sail from Acapulco.'

Lord Yelverton looked as he spoke at Ajax Audenshaw and he knew that while his eyes were on the carvings he held in the palm of his hand, he was listening intently.

'When he reached Acapulco the Spaniard was just about to embark when he became ill,' Lord Yelverton went on. 'He missed the ship which was to carry him home to Spain, and when he was well enough to continue his journey, he found there would be some delay before he could find another that was prepared to accept passengers.'

Ajax Audenshaw smiled.

'It must have been quite a problem in

those days. Go on!'

'He therefore became greedy and thought he would return North to increase the treasure he already had with him.'

'I am beginning to see where this story leads,' Audenshaw remarked.

'It is really quite simple,' Lord Yelverton agreed. 'He trusted one family to hide his treasures in one of the caves in the hills just above here. He then, in typically cruel fashion, extracted from them a vow of silence, and to make sure they kept it, sacrificed their eldest son to make his spirit the guardian of the treasure, until he should return.'

Audenshaw nodded and said:

'They were too superstitious not to believe that if they stole or revealed to anyone what the soul of their son was guarding, he would suffer for all eternity.'

The story had been told by Lord Yelverton in an almost expressionless voice but now as Audenshaw understood, his eyes lit up.

'How was the seaman aware of this?'

'He told me that the secret of the Spanish treasure had been handed down through his family for generations,' Lord Yelverton said, 'but he was the last of the line. He had left Mexico during the Revolution but before he went he had killed a local man of importance and knew he could never come back. He had therefore stolen four objects from the cave where they had been hidden for nearly three hundred years and had already sold two pieces in Egypt.'

Audenshaw groaned, but he did not interrupt as Lord Yelverton went on:

'I had no intention at that time of coming to Mexico, but with these in my possession I had no choice.'

'No, of course not.'

'And you will help me?'

There was an obvious pause while he felt his fate hung in the balance. Then to his surprise Ajax Audenshaw lying back in his chair, opened his mouth and shouted.

His voice seemed to boom out almost like the break of the waves on the shore.

'Tula! Come here, Tula!' he yelled.

There was a moment's silence. Then Audenshaw roared again:

'Tula! Tula! Where the hell are you?'

A quiet voice just behind them replied: 'I am here.'

'Then why do you not say so?' Audenshaw asked.

On to the verandah through the open window came a girl who to Lord Yelverton's surprise, looked completely different from anyone he had expected.

When Audenshaw had called her name he had expected because Tula had been the capital of the Toltec territory, a native.

Instead of a Mexican with bronzed skin and dark hair, the girl he saw was fair and there was a slight resemblance to Audenshaw, which made him sure he was her father.

There was more gold in her hair than in his and it had red lights in it, which gave the impression of flames ignited by the sun.

But her eyes were blue, the deep blue of the sea which lay in front of them, and under a loose gown of blue cotton he had the impression that her body was as shapely and supple as Carlotta's ebony figure he had seen posing when he first arrived.

'What is it you want, Papa?' Tula enquired softly and Audenshaw held out his hand.

When she saw what lay in his palm she gave a little cry that was one of sheer delight.

'Wherever did you get them?' she asked. 'They are lovely! Quite perfect! And of course Mixtec.'

'That is what I thought,' Audenshaw agreed, 'and you must show our guest the piece you have of crystal.'

As if she noticed him for the first time, Tula looked at Lord Yelverton and he saw what he thought was a surprising expression of resentment on her face, as if she had no wish to share her treasures with him.

'This is Lord Yelverton,' her father explained. 'He brought me these with the story that they had come from a cave in the hills behind us, left there by a Spaniard who looted them from Monte Albán.'

He looked at Lord Yelverton and added:

'By the way, I did not hear what happened to him.'

'According to my informant he never came back,' Lord Yelverton replied. 'I presume he either died in Mexico City, or other tomb-robbers murdered him.'

'Or perhaps their guardians disposed of him,' Ajax Audenshaw remarked. 'These things do happen, as Tula will tell you.'

The girl said nothing, and once again Lord Yelverton thought she was resenting him.

'What do you intend to do about it, Papa?' she enquired.

'What do you expect me to do?' her

father countered. 'I have promised Dolores that I will not leave her to go on any more expeditions.'

'If you are talking about me,' a voice said in Spanish, 'I want to hear what you are saying.'

The voice was low and exotic and Lord Yelverton rose as he saw a vision of loveliness come out onto the verandah.

She was obviously Spanish with large, dark eyes which flashed as she spoke, in an olive-hued oval face.

She had a red mouth that was made for kisses or for pouting to get her own way, and a voluptuous body which would doubtless be fat when she grew older, but for the moment was enticingly provocative.

She was dressed in the silks, frills and furbelows which the Spanish, and especially the Mexican-Spanish, found irresistible, and she wore a necklace of pearls which encircled the golden column of her neck, while pearls and diamonds glittered in her small ears.

She was like a bird of Paradise and Lord Yelverton was not surprised when Ajax Audenshaw put out his hand towards her, and there was an expression in his eyes that was undisguisedly one of desire.

'You are not leaving,' Dolores said. 'You know that I cannot live without you.'

The passion in her voice was unmistakable.

'I am not leaving, my adorable one,' Audenshaw replied.

Lord Yelverton glanced at Tula and wondered what she thought of his behaviour.

He saw she was paying no attention to it, but only staring at the mystic carvings which she now held in her hand.

She stood on the edge of the verandah so that the light from the sun fell on them and Lord Yelverton felt she was entirely unconscious of anything that was happening behind her.

'Good! Then that is settled!' Dolores said with satisfaction, 'and this *Señor* can go away—how do you say?—with a flea in his ear!'

Audenshaw laughed. Then he said:

'That would be very impolite when he has travelled all the way from Mexico City to meet me.'

'There are plenty of people he can talk to about dead bones and the days that are gone and forgotten. I am interested only in what lives, and breathes today—and of course, tonight!'

The look she gave Audenshaw was very revealing and Lord Yelverton thought it was almost as if they made love to each other in public.

Embarrassed, he walked across to Tula.

'What do you think of them?' he asked.

He thought there was a moment's pause before his voice penetrated her concentration. Then she said surprisingly:

'They are lovely, but I sense that where they came from is sacred and should be left untouched.'

'You cannot mean that!' Lord Yelverton

asked in astonishment.

Tula put the two objects she held in her hand into his.

'I think, My Lord,' she said clearly and distinctly, 'that your journey here has been wasted.'

2

Sitting at the big Dining-Room table with the Mexican servants in their white and red clothes, waiting on them, Lord Yelverton thought it was the strangest party at which he had ever been a guest.

He had been wondering what he should say to Tula and how he would answer her strange statement, when there was the sound of high voices and what seemed to him a whole school of children burst onto the verandah all talking at once.

They greeted Ajax Audenshaw affectionately and ignored Dolores, who when they appeared looked at them with dislike, then stalked back into the house.

Only Tula seemed prepared to attend to them and give orders.

'Go and wash your hands,' she said.

'Supper will be ready in ten minutes and, Lucette, tidy your hair. It looks a mess.'

The girl she addressed, who Lord Yelverton thought was about thirteen years of age, tossed her head rebelliously, but a moment later left the verandah apparently to do as she was told.

It struck Lord Yelverton with surprise that the children were addressing Ajax Audenshaw as 'Papa', and he thought it must be just a figure of speech, and they could not really all be his children.

It was only when they sat down to dinner that he discovered he was wrong.

They were all in fact, the Englishman's offspring, and he gradually gathered during the evening that their mothers had stayed with the archaeologist, or painter, however one chose to describe him, for a year or so, then departed leaving the result of their union behind.

The most recent member of the family was only two and would therefore not appear at the evening meal, but the rest were the strangest collection Lord Yelverton had ever seen.

But first as the children clustered round him, Audenshaw had said to his guest:

'I expect after your journey you would like a bath. The servants will prepare one for you, but do not be too long or my children will be so hungry they will be prepared to eat you as well as everything else they can lay their hands on.'

'You intend me to stay with you?' Lord Yelverton asked.

'Why not?' Audenshaw replied. 'You will be far more comfortable than camping on the beach. Tula will show you to your room.'

Lord Yelverton followed Tula through a maze of passages towards another part of the house and he had the feeling as he did so, that she was not only resenting that he was to stay with them, but also disliking him.

It was something he had not often encountered in his life and he found himself intrigued as to why he should have this effect on a young girl who he thought might have welcomed another man in a household that was obviously dominated by her father.

When they reached what he realized was a quiet room where the windows opened out onto a magnificent view of the sea, she said:

'I expect your own servants will bring you everything you require, I will send someone to show them where you are sleeping.'

'Thank you.'

She paused as if she had something else to say to him but was not certain how to put it into words.

Then, as if she could not help herself, she said:

'Please do not upset Papa by making him feel home-sick.'

'Home-sick!' Lord Yelverton exclaimed.

'He often longs for England, but it would be a mistake for him to return there and his...responsibilities are here.'

He knew by the way she hesitated over the word 'responsibilities' that she meant herself and the children he had seen. Since he was not yet sure of their position in Ajax Audenshaw's life, he asked lightly:

'Does he really, with his vast knowledge of antiquity, enjoy the simple role of *"pater familias"* with apparently nothing else to do but paint?'

He knew as he spoke that Tula thought his question impertinent and her blue eyes seemed almost to flash at him as she replied:

'It is the life Papa has chosen and I wish him to be happy.'

She did not wait for Lord Yelverton's reply but turned away and left, shutting the door somewhat sharply behind her.

He smiled as he listened to her footsteps moving away down the uncarpeted passage.

Then he looked around his room with appreciation.

It was certainly more comfortable than

the tent in which he had slept for the last five nights, and he felt the conversation he would have with his host would be decidedly more stimulating than any he had enjoyed in the villages in which he had camped.

At the same time he was still puzzled and intrigued by what he had seen of Ajax Audenshaw, finding it hard to believe that his distinction as an archaeologist could be set aside so lightly for what seemed a wasteful existence of indolence and womanizing.

He was however, certainly delighted to be provided with a large bed that looked comfortable, a room well furnished with colourful native rugs on a polished floor, and furniture which gave evidence of craftsmen who were experts at their calling.

What both surprised and delighted Lord Yelverton was that opening out of his bedroom there was a bath.

It was something he had not expected,

and although it was somewhat primitive, the shower, manipulated cleverly from the ceiling, washed away the dust of his journey and made him feel both cool and refreshed.

It was still early in the evening, but he put on the evening-clothes which he always wore when he travelled which were conventional except that his shirt did not have a stiff front and his collar was slightly lower than he would have worn at a more formal party.

He looked exceedingly elegant when his man-servant who had been with him for many years and in many countries had finished ministering to him, and he walked back the way he had come with Tula.

He learned where the rest of the party was waiting for him from the noise the children were making, and now as he reached them on the verandah outside the large windows of what he realized was the Dining-Room, he saw Ajax Audenshaw was also in evening-clothes.

His were strangely colourful in a style more Mexican than English, especially the embroidered jacket and the glittering stripes on the long black trousers.

They made him appear more handsome and more raffish than he had before, and Lord Yelverton could understand why Dolores looked at him with smouldering eyes, as he was certain a great number of women were always ready to do.

The children, whose ages appeared to run from Lucette at thirteen to the twins who must have been approximately six or seven, had all changed into light cotton dresses if they were girls, or Mexican dress if they were boys.

They were all very different in appearance, and at the same time so colourful that Lord Yelverton felt almost as if he was at a children's Fancy Dress party.

Only Tula was conventional in a white gown that was very plain and simply cut, and yet seemed somehow to make her look different in a manner Lord Yelverton could not explain.

The deep gold of her hair, the dark blue of her eyes, the fairness of her skin reminded him, he thought, of a young Greek goddess rising from the foam of the sea.

But there was something else, something he did not understand, which despite the aloof manner in which she treated him, made him want to know more about her.

There was a long, cool drink of fruit juice and native rum which Lord Yelverton found delicious.

Then a servant announced that the meal was ready.

There was a shriek of delight from the children and they would all have rushed into the Dining-Room if a sharp word from Tula had not made them wait until she and Dolores had walked in first followed by their father and Lord Yelverton.

Dolores had taken the opportunity afforded by having a visitor present to deck herself in all her finery.

Her frilled dress in the same red as the Hibiscus flowers, was ornamented with a profusion of jewellery and her scarf of orchid purple chiffon gave her an Oriental look.

Although she displayed for Audenshaw a voluptuousness which was rather embarrassing to watch, she could not help giving Lord Yelverton occasionally provocative glances from under her long eye-lashes and smiling as if she offered him many delightful pleasures should he be brave enough to demand them.

Audenshaw sat at the head of the table with Dolores on his right and indicated a chair at his left hand side for Lord Yelverton to occupy.

Tula was at the other end of the table and the children pushed and shoved themselves into the first chair that was nearest to them.

It was only when they were all seated that Lord Yelverton looking at them noticed that they all seemed to have a remarkable resemblance to Ajax Audenshaw.

Lucette was obviously French, there was no doubt about that, but her straight nose and her firm chin were almost identical to those of the man she called *'mon Père'*.

The twins, although they were obviously Mexican to look at, had blue eyes which were astonishingly vivid, against their dark skin, and two other little girls, one with distinctive Chinese features, the other who might, Lord Yelverton thought, have had a Brazilian mother had also characteristics that could be easily ascribed to their father.

There was one boy of about twelve, who seemed somewhat aggressive and bullied the younger children, and another one perhaps nine years old, who had nothing to say but spent his time making bread pellets which he flicked across the table when Tula was not looking.

The children were unselfconscious and

obviously not the least shy, and they chatted amongst themselves and occasionally to Tula, and tried to catch their father's attention, who behaved as if they were not there.

Instead he concentrated on talking to Lord Yelverton telling him stories that he found extremely fascinating, about the excavations in which he had taken part before he wrote his book on the Aztecs.

Dolores was bored when the conversation did not concern herself and because Audenshaw was interested in Lord Yelverton, she obviously resented him, saying crossly halfway through dinner:

'You are not to speak to Ajax so much about all that is dead and gone. Now he lives in the present, and with me.'

'He may do that,' Lord Yelverton replied, 'but he is still one of the greatest experts in the world on the history of this country and wherever Aztec ruins are to be found.'

'They are dead—dead—dead!' Dolores

flashed, 'and I am alive, am I not, my loved one?'

She put her ringed hand as she spoke over Ajax's.

He smiled at her and without bothering to reply continued his conversation with Lord Yelverton.

Somewhat to the latter's surprise, the food was delicious and not Mexican which, prepared always with strong spices, he had found monotonous on his journey.

Now he ate with relish the lobsters, fresh that morning from the caves beneath them and the red snapper caught in the nets Audenshaw's fisherman trawled in his own bay.

The chicken and rice which followed for once was not covered with a sauce guaranteed to set a man's stomach on fire.

The menu ended with fruit which came to the table in large native woven wicker baskets.

There were papaya and melons, coconuts

and pineapples which Lord Yelverton had seen ripe in the fields as they neared Acapulco.

As soon as they had finished dinner the children asked if they could leave and with their voices rising with excitement on being free, they rushed out through the open window, leaving a silence behind them.

For a moment Tula sat on the far end of the table. Then she too rose and Lord Yelverton looked towards her, wondering if she would join them.

Instead she said in a quiet voice:

'I hope you will excuse me, Papa. I have things to see to. Would you like your coffee on the verandah?'

'No, we will have it here,' Ajax Audenshaw replied. 'I find it easier to talk with the table beneath my elbows.'

'The chairs are more comfortable on the verandah,' Dolores pouted.

Audenshaw ignored her, continuing his conversation with Lord Yelverton and telling him so many interesting things that they forgot that Dolores was present until she rose and flounced away, furious at being ignored.

Finally as the sun was sinking in a blaze of glory they went out onto the verandah.

Dolores was swinging backwards and forwards on a native swing made of bamboo and obviously sulking.

Ajax Audenshaw walked across to her, pulled her into his arms, kissed her roughly and passionately, then pushed her onto the swing again.

'I am cross with you!' she said.

'I know,' he replied, 'but you must learn that men have mental needs besides physical ones, and must wait your turn.'

He smiled as he spoke and it took the sting out of the words.

Then as if she could not help herself Dolores giggled.

'You are an infuriating man,' she said, 'and I cannot think why I love you.'

'I will give you the answer to that later,'

Ajax Audenshaw replied.

He settled himself down in a comfortable chair beside Lord Yelverton and went on talking where he had left off.

While they talked they sipped a local liqueur which was sweet and tasted of strawberries, but nonetheless was quite potent.

Lord Yelverton began to feel a little sleepy and at the same time, mellow and at peace with the world.

He did not know what he had expected to find on his arrival, but Audenshaw's household was certainly different from anything he could have imagined.

At the same time it was interesting and amusing.

Finally in response to a restlessness from Dolores which was impossible to ignore, Audenshaw rose to his feet. Lord Yelverton also was ready to go to bed.

'We will talk again in the morning,' his host said, 'and I usually swim before breakfast. Join me if you feel like it.'

'At what time?' Lord Yelverton enquired.

'When the sun rises at about seven o'clock.'

'It will be something I shall look forward to and thank you for allowing me to be your guest.'

'I have enjoyed this evening,' Ajax Audenshaw said simply.

As he spoke Lord Yelverton saw a frightened expression in Dolores' eyes as she felt that already he was escaping from her clutches and she might lose him.

When Audenshaw had left, Lord Yelverton after drinking the last remaining drops of the liqueur that was in his glass, thought he should go to bed.

Then instead of going into the house he walked down from the verandah over the sparse grass of what was intended to be a lawn.

He knew it was only kept from being scorched back into the sand in which it grew by being frequently watered, but the hibiscus bushes on either side of it were bright with flowers and coconut trees soaring against the sky were heavy with fruit.

Since they had finished dinner the stars had come out in the vast darkness of the sky, and there was also a half moon which threw its light over the sea, touching the softly undulating water with silver.

It was so exquisitely beautiful that Lord Yelverton felt as if he had stepped into another world, one which had nothing in common with the rush and bustle of cities and the increasing greed of man for money in whatever way he could obtain it.

He walked on until he found himself on the edge of a cliff not very high above the sandy bay below, and with some roughly cut steps winding downwards.

The waves were just lapping against the sand. It was the only sound to be heard and so soft that one had to listen for it.

Then as Lord Yelverton stood looking out to where the stars ended in the indecisive horizon he was aware that he was not alone.

A little to the left of him between two palm trees growing almost on the cliff's edge he saw a slight figure.

In a white gown with the moonlight on her fair hair and her face turned upwards towards the stars, he thought at first that she looked like a young goddess as she had when he had first seen her.

But now she was more like a figure-head on the great wooden Spanish ships that had once sailed through the seas below, bringing men to conquer and destroy a culture and a people whose amazing civilization had thus been lost for all time.

Quietly Lord Yelverton moved towards Tula and only when he stood beside her was she aware that he was there.

He knew in some strange, perceptive way that she had been so deep in her thoughts, so concentrated on another world than the one in which she was living, that as he jerked her back into the present, she hated him almost violently.

Then surprising himself by his words he said:

'Was it of Quetzalcoatl you were thinking?'

He knew as he spoke that he startled her, and she turned her head to look at him. In the moonlight he could see the astonishment on her face.

Then she asked:

'Why should you...expect that I was... thinking of...him?'

Lord Yelverton smiled.

'It has only recently been discovered that the Pyramid to Quetzalcoatl attested the grandeur of Tula.'

'Yes...of course.'

He thought she was almost reading his thoughts and guessed he had a deeper reason than what he had indicated aloud.

Then Lord Yelverton asked:

'Have you studied the cult of the Plumed Serpent?'

For a moment Tula was still. Then she said in a strange voice:

'Why do you speak to me of such things? What has my father told you about me?'

'We have not discussed you at all,' Lord Yelverton replied, 'but your name is Tula and the way you looked at my treasures and your disinclination to help me, tells me that you feel I am an intruder in something that belongs to you.'

She made a compulsive little gesture and clasped her hands together, but she did not speak. After a moment Lord Yelverton said:

'That is true, is it not? You resent me because you think I might find out too much, because you are keeping a secret that you believe is too sacred for those who approach the past with curiosity and not with awe.'

There was a long silence while Tula did not answer him. Then after a moment she said almost as if she wished to convince herself:

'You are...curious. Surely that is...all?'

'No,' Lord Yelverton replied. 'If that had been all, I should have gone to Monte Albán and taken part in the excavations there.'

'Perhaps you...think that what you will...find here is more...valuable.'

'I am not interested in the monetary value or any fame I might win for having found it.'

'Then...what do you...want?'

The question was sharp and now Tula turned round to face him defiantly.

Lord Yelverton's eyes met hers. Then it was as if they battled with the vibrations that flowed between them rather than with weapons.

As if he allowed her to conquer him for the moment he replied:

'I will tell you why I have come. I did not mean to tell anybody, not even your father, but because you compel me I will speak the truth.'

She did not move as he spoke, she did

not even draw herself up. Yet he felt in some way that she sat in judgement upon him and only if he made out a good case for himself would she help him to attain what he desired.

Because he was very reserved he found it difficult to find words in which to express himself. Then he said:

'Perhaps it will not seem as strange to you as it did to me, but the moment the Mexican seaman put the jaguar bone into my hands it made me feel that it was different from anything I had ever touched before.'

'In what...way?'

He could hardly hear the words, and yet they were spoken.

'If I say it was a vibration, that is not the right word, but something emanated from it which only you will understand. When I was able to translate some of the words and pictures on the carving I knew that the bone was dedicated to Quetzalcoatl and had been used in the worship of him.'

'You could not have known that!'

'I knew!' Lord Yelverton insisted. 'Or should I say I felt it?'

'What...else?'

'As soon as I reached England I studied all that was known of Quetzalcoatl, god of the wind, life and the morning star.'

Tula did not speak and Lord Yelverton went on quietly:

'He also taught the movement of the stars, and I think that was what you were looking at just now, and trying to find in them his message because of what he means to you.'

'Stop!'

The words seemed to burst from between Tula's lips.

Then she said angrily:

'I cannot...believe you are saying this to me, because you...have thought of it yourself. Someone must have...told you what to say...before you arrived.'

Lord Yelverton shook his head.

'I do not suppose you will believe me,'

he said, 'but I had no intention before my arrival of speaking to your father or anyone else of what I felt about Quetzalcoatl. I came to find the tomb merely because of the bone and the amber, and I hope to discover more pieces.'

He paused before he said slowly:

'If there are more, I know they too will prove to be dedicated to Quetzalcoatl with whom, although I cannot understand it, I feel I have a kind of affinity.'

Tula made an inaudible little sound and turned to look once again out to sea.

'I have told you the truth,' Lord Yelverton concluded, 'and I must add that I am extremely surprised at myself for speaking of such intimate matters. At the same time, I know that you understand.'

'I do not...wish to do...so,' Tula said in a low voice. 'Go away and...leave me...alone! I do not want you...here!'

'It is too late,' Lord Yelverton replied. 'I am here and whether you like it or not, you are aware that we have something in common which neither of us has with anyone else.'

She lifted her chin a little as he spoke.

He thought with a faint flicker of amusement that she was resenting his presumption in assuming he was the only person in her life who could talk to her of such matters.

Yet he was sure that was the truth. He was the only person who had ever talked to her of things she had hidden deep in her heart.

Now almost as if he had violated her, she was shocked and angry that he had encroached on something that to her was sacred.

As if she had spoken he said:

'It is too late to send me away. I am here, and because I think you know it is fate and there is nothing either of us can do about it, you must help me.'

'Why should I do...that?'

She spoke defiantly and he felt sure that she was still fighting to be rid of him.

'I will give you two reasons,' he said. 'First, because you now know that this tomb exists, and secondly, because it concerns Quetzalcoatl you are curious about it, but you are too honest to send me away and then investigate for yourself.'

'You are presuming a great deal about me, My Lord,' Tula said bitterly. 'I can tell you nothing and why should I?'

'As I saw you here, something outside myself told me what you were thinking and doing as you stood staring up at the stars.'

He paused before he went on:

'At first I thought that you looked like a figure-head on one of the great Spanish ships that used to sail into the harbour. Then I knew you did not arrive with them but you were here centuries before they came to pillage and destroy.'

His voice was very quiet as he went on:

'Perhaps you were there when Quetzal-coatl was forced by the trickery of another deity to leave his home in Tula. Perhaps you too were disturbed by evil omens for which the Priests and sorcerers could find no satisfactory explanation.'

Tula made a restless movement as if she would prevent him from saying any more, but he went on:

'Do you remember the column of fire in the east at midnight which shone every night for an entire year? Do you recall huge comets with fiery tails shooting through the sky in the daytime?'

'No...do not say any more!' Tula begged in a whisper, but he continued:

'Did you see the waters of the lake churned to a frenzy when not even a breeze was blowing and hear the voice of a woman wailing in the night?'

He saw Tula shiver, then as she put up her hands to her face Lord Yelverton said quietly:

'I am sure just now you were wondering if Quetzalcoatl could keep his promise that one day he would return.'

★ ★ ★ ★

Later that night when Lord Yelverton lay in the comfortable bed in his room and saw the moonlight flooding in through the uncurtained windows, he wondered if, in fact, he had, when he was talking to Tula, become a little mad.

He tried to tell himself it was the effect of the wines he had drunk at dinner, and especially the liqueur.

Never in the whole of his restrained, controlled and organized life had he allowed himself to behave in such a strange manner or let words which were not his own come into his mind and pass through his lips without his conscious volition.

He thought that any other woman would have laughed and told him he was 'tipsy', but Tula had merely shuddered.

He had known from her frightened whispers and the strange expression in her eyes that she was afraid because he was speaking not only his own thoughts but hers.

'I was bewitched!' Lord Yelverton told himself, 'but by whom? Certainly not by Tula, who had obviously no wish to listen to what I was saying, but had not the strength to escape from me.'

She had sat down on the ground as if her legs would no longer carry her, and asked him piteously:

'How...can you know...all this? Not even Papa...knows the things of which you have just...spoken. What books are there in England that can...describe matters that here are...secret?'

For a moment Lord Yelverton did not move. Then he too sat down and found there was a coconut tree behind him against which he could lean.

'I do not know from where my knowledge comes,' he replied. 'I do not know why I said it to you, but no-one had told it to me nor have I read it. Suddenly it was there in my mind and on my lips.'

Tula drew in her breath and he saw that her fingers were clasped together almost convulsively.

'It is certainly uncanny,' he said ruminatively. 'Perhaps we are bewitched!'

'You are English!' Tula exclaimed, as if that made it impossible.

'I suppose now I think of it,' he continued, 'the jaguar bone and the amber have exerted a strange influence on me ever since I first possessed them.'

'In what...way?'

'I have always been conscious of them and I have felt reluctant to leave them, even at night, out of contact with me.'

She did not reply and he went on:

'In the daytime I have carried them in my pocket. At night, telling myself it was because I was afraid they might be stolen, I have kept them under my pillow.'

There was silence for quite some time. Then he said:

'I think now you have made up your mind.'

She made a gesture with her hands that was very expressive.

'You are...trying to read my...thoughts!'

'I am reading them,' he said. 'You will help me because you feel it is the right thing to do, and fate has sent me to you, or perhaps Quetzalcoatl himself!'

'You are not to mock him.'

'Do you really think I am doing that?' Lord Yelverton enquired. 'If I mock at anybody it will be at myself. I am a staid, reserved English archaeologist, one who has always had his feet firmly on the ground, concerned only with the history of the objects he had found.'

'You know that is not...true.'

Tula did not say it as if it was a compliment, but almost as if she disparaged the manner in which he was trying to mock at himself.

'It was true until now,' he replied.

Quite suddenly he felt as if the whole

thing was intolerable and that he must quite unawares, have become the victim of some trickery that he could not identify.

He rose to his feet saying:

'I think I should go to bed. Perhaps things will seem clearer and more sensible in the morning.'

Tula did not answer. She merely turned her face towards the stars as if she was pretending he was not there.

He stood looking for a long moment at the moonlight on her face and the light of the stars which seemed somehow to have been caught in the darkness of her eyes.

Then as if the sight of her gave him no pleasure he turned and walked away back into the house.

He saw no-one and everything was very quiet.

He had told his man-servant not to wait up for him and as he took off his clothes and flung them down on a chair he was certain that he was deluding himself in a way that he found extremely reprehensible because it concerned his work.

He had always despised the archaeologists who tried to make capital out of their findings by pretending there was a curse attributed to some tomb they had opened or that the treasures they unearthed would bring good fortune to those who acquired them.

It was only a way, Lord Yelverton had said often enough, of extracting money from the gullible.

He was concerned only with facts, palatable or unpalatable. But he had tonight, crossed the barrier between the real and the fantastic in a manner which made him ashamed of himself.

'I must have been drunk without knowing it,' he thought.

But he knew when he spoke such strange words, he was entirely clear-headed, and while he was speaking to Tula in such a strange manner she had seemed to him only a young woman who was being tiresome in not agreeing immediately to help him as he wished her to in his pursuit of the past.

'Quetzalcoatl who is a dead and forgotten god, means nothing to me,' he said to himself. 'What I am interested in are the objects which might have been dedicated to him, but which came from the Mixtec Empire.'

The discovery of more carvings of mythical scenes would be of benefit to all students of history in the future.

'That is why I am here,' Lord Yelverton said positively.

But even as he heard his own voice in the moonlit bedroom, he knew he lied.

3

Lord Yelverton woke early and lay for some time thinking.

Then he rose and putting on his bathing-shorts found that beside them there was a robe made of white Turkish towelling.

Wearing a pair of heel-less slippers he wandered through the passages and out onto the verandah where he found not his host as he had expected, but a servant waiting for him.

'*Señor* say go down beach,' he said.

Lord Yelverton nodded a reply and walked through the coconut trees and hibiscus shrubs as he had last night, then down the twisting steps which led to the sands below.

Inevitably he found his thoughts returning to Tula and his strange conversation with her in the moonlight, and now he told himself that what he had said was so uncharacteristic that he must in fact, have been drunk. There could be no other explanation.

'I was tired after a long day's riding,' he explained to himself, 'and the liqueur was obviously far more potent than it seemed.'

He ignored the fact that he had a very strong head and that apart from the liqueur, he had drunk very little compared with the amount of wine he would have enjoyed at a dinner-party at home.

Ajax Audenshaw was waiting for him. He looked so magnificently strong that despite his age he was a sight to make any woman's heart beat quicker.

'Good-morning, Yelverton! Have a good night?' he asked casually.

'I slept peacefully thanks to your extremely comfortable bed,' Lord Yelverton replied.

'Good! If you are ready to take the water

you will find it surprisingly warm.'

'I am looking forward to it.'

It was the sort of conversation any two Englishmen might have had anywhere in the world, and Lord Yelverton thought that it swept away his anxieties regarding his behaviour of the night before.

There was no doubt at all that he had been talking nonsense becuase he had drunk too much.

Ajax Audenshaw was like a porpoise in the water and Lord Yelverton, though a good swimmer, found it hard to keep up with him.

They swam a long way out to sea, then turning simultaneously, trod water to look back at the land behind them.

The sun, golden and compelling, had risen to give a dazzling gleam to the hills above the harbour and behind them again to the mountains in the distance.

The whole vista was so lovely that Lord Yelverton could only stare at it spellbound, until beside him Audenshaw said:

'Now you understand why I am content to live here.'

'It is one of the loveliest places I have ever seen, but I am surprised that someone with your brain finds it enough.'

'I have my painting.'

Lord Yelverton did not reply. He only started to swim slowly back towards the beach and his host swam beside him.

Only when they stepped out onto the golden sand to feel the sun warm on their wet bodies did Audenshaw say almost as if Lord Yelverton had accused him of indolence:

'I have been thinking of writing a book on the Toltecs.'

The word brought Tula instantly to Lord Yelverton's mind and he remembered how she had asked him not to make her father homesick.

Because he felt it was her fault he had been so unrestrained he said deliberately:

'I would like you to see my recent findings in Egypt, and I am sure there is a great deal more there that has not yet been located.'

Ajax Audenshaw looked interested.

Then as Lord Yelverton talked of the tomb he had excavated he said:

'I decided some time ago not to return to Europe. My place is here.'

This Lord Yelverton thought was true, yet wishing to defy Tula he said:

'I think it is a mistake to be confined to one particular part of the world, when there is so much to see, and fortunately so much to do, in many different places.'

'You are tempting me!' Audenshaw complained.

While they were talking they had put on the white towelling robes and divested themselves of their wet bathing trunks.

They left them to dry in the sun and walked up the steps towards the house.

'Breakfast in five minutes,' Audenshaw said, as they stepped onto the verandah.

Lord Yelverton went to his own room and as he did so he heard Audenshaw shouting to the servants to hurry with the food.

Lord Yelverton was surprised when some minutes later he found breakfast waiting on the verandah but no-one else there except Ajax Audenshaw.

'Where are the children?' he asked.

'At school,' their father replied. 'They start work early in Mexico and fortunately we have some retired teachers living in the village, who can teach Lucette the things I wish her to know.'

There was a proprietory note in his voice which somehow surprised Lord Yelverton.

It seemed strange that a man who could be so promiscuous and have so many women in his life could also concern himself in a conscientious, paternal manner with the education of his illegitimate children.

'And where is *Señora* Dolores?' Lord Yelverton asked.

If she had another name he had never heard it.

His host laughed.

'Dolores is Spanish and if you can get her out of bed before midday you would be a magician.'

There was a third place laid at the table which Lord Yelverton then knew was for Tula, and as if his thought of her conjured her up, at that moment she came onto the verandah.

She bent and kissed her father's cheek as she passed his chair, then sat down at the table giving Lord Yelverton only a slight inclination of her head as he rose to stand until she was seated.

'Where have you been?' Ajax Audenshaw enquired.

'I have been with Petronella,' Tula replied. 'She is still teething and Joanna tells me passed a restless night.'

'I will go and see her.'

'She is asleep now. I have made her some herbs and mixed them with honey, and I think she will feel better when she wakes.'

It was a conversation, Lord Yelverton thought, that might have taken place in any suburban home in England, and he found it strange simply because it was so out of context in such an exotic setting, between two such unusual people.

'My youngest daughter I am convinced is not strong, although Tula disagrees with me,' Audenshaw said to Lord Yelverton.

'She is fretful and because she has had trouble with her teeth,' Tula said sharply.

'She is fretful because she is like her mother,' Audenshaw replied. 'A tiresome woman, undeniably beautiful, but at the same time eternally worrying over trifles which are not of the least importance.'

Lord Yelverton wanted to laugh, but he felt it would be impolite and with difficulty controlled himself.

'I am going to paint,' Audenshaw said. 'Carlotta should be here by now, and incidentally, Tula, she is the best model I have had for a very long time.'

'If you tell her so, she will demand more

money!' Tula replied.

'She has already done that,' her father answered. 'I have told her she must keep to her contract, but actually she does not know what I mean by that. Like all women she believes the more pleasure she gives the more she should be paid.'

He smiled as he moved away from the table. Then as he reached the door into the house he turned to say:

'If you two are going to explore, do not forget to let the servants know if you will be back tonight or if you will be camping out. I dislike having to wait unnecessarily for my dinner.'

He did not wait for an answer but disappeared and Lord Yelverton looked at Tula.

'Are we going exploring?'

'You have not changed your mind?'

'You know I am not likely to do that. At the same time I feel I should apologize to you for the nonsense I talked last night.'

She raised her eyebrows as if this was

94

something she had not expected him to say. Then she asked in a low voice:

'Was it...nonsense?'

'It was the combination of a long journey and a very potent liqueur.'

'Of course! That is the inevitable explanation made by an Englishman who thinks he has made a fool of himself!'

She was mocking him which amazed him. But he had no wish to quarrel with her, knowing that he needed her help.

There was silence. Then as if Tula made up her mind, she said:

'Very well. We will ride in the direction I think you want to go, but I do not wish to raise your hopes too high. It may be impossible to...find what you...seek.'

Lord Yelverton looked at her sharply.

'What you are saying is that I may be prevented from finding it.'

'That is certainly one interpretation.'

'I have no choice,' he said quietly, 'except to throw myself on your mercy.

I am well aware that without your help I am powerless.'

Tula drew in her breath.

'Why must you be so greedy?' she asked in a very different tone. 'You have obtained unexpectedly what most collectors would be extremely grateful to own. Why not be content?'

Lord Yelverton smiled a little cynically.

'Would you be?' he asked, 'and would you not despise me if I was so faint-hearted, or shall I say weak-willed, to turn back now I have come so far and am in fact, within reach of my goal.'

He saw by the expression on Tula's face that she was still very unsympathetic and he asked angrily:

'Why must you appoint yourself as the angel with the flaming sword, brandishing it outside the Garden of Eden to prevent me from entering?'

'It is not...I who would...prevent you,' Tula said in a low voice.

'Then who?'

She did not reply and after a moment he said:

'Are you referring to the living, or the dead? Surely this morning, sitting in the sunlight at breakfast, that most prosaic meal, we cannot still be bewitched as we undoubtedly were last night. Or was it a case of moon-madness?'

There was no doubt that his tone was scathing as he said the last words and abruptly Tula pushed back her chair.

'I will order the horses, My Lord,' she said, 'and we will leave in ten minutes' time. But you must come alone.'

'I shall be ready,' Lord Yelverton replied.

He felt a surge of satisfaction that he had got his own way.

It was almost as if he had battled with forces that were far stronger than one slim young woman and had been the victor.

As he went to his room he wondered why she was being so difficult.

Was it to show her power? Or perhaps

like all women she wished to be mysterious, just for the hell of it!

Lord Yelverton told himself he must be wary and see that she did not trick him.

It would be easy to show him an empty cave and say it was the one he had sought but it had been cleaned out by robbers or perhaps by earlier archaeologists.

He remembered that the seaman had told him the cave was near a cascade, and he thought that as he had not mentioned this to Tula it would be a test of whether she was taking him to the right place.

'I do not trust her,' he told himself, and wished that he could have persuaded Ajax Audenshaw to come with him.

It was maddening to think of him wasting his remarkable talent as an archaeologist, painting pictures which would not be admired by Academicians or the majority of the public.

Lord Yelverton however, had the uneasy feeling that there was nevertheless a touch of genius about them.

If that was true, they might prevent Audenshaw from returning to his archaeological research and his book on the Toltecs would never be written.

Then he told himself cynically that when Dolores began to bore Audenshaw, doubtless his passion for painting would fade at the same time.

It was unlikely the Spanish woman would last very long, for judging by the amatory mile-stones in the persons of his children, none of his love-affairs exceeded two to three years.

Then there would be new faces, new interests and perhaps he might even be persuaded to come to Egypt.

Lord Yelverton felt pleased at the thought.

Eccentric though he might be, he liked Audenshaw, and he also had a great respect for his knowledge and ability, which he knew now that he had talked to him, were unsurpassed by any other archaeologist in the world.

'He cannot stay here for long founding a family and ignoring his responsibility to future generations as an exceptionally gifted interpreter of the past,' Lord Yelverton told himself.

He decided that when he came back from his expedition with Tula, he would have a long talk with her father and try to make him see sense.

He had the feeling she would bitterly oppose him in this as she had tried to thwart him in his desire to find the cave.

He would therefore give her no inkling of his intention otherwise he thought apprehensively, she might make things more difficult for him than she was doing at the moment.

Ready, he went to the front of the house to find, as he expected his horse waiting for him and Tula already mounted on one of the sturdy young ponies which the Mexicans found were sure-footed and capable of long hours of endurance when ridden over the mountains.

He looked at Tula and saw with astonishment that she was sitting astride.

Granted she was wearing the fringed suede divided skirt that had been invented in South America and which always looked extremely attractive on the wearer.

But that, Lord Yelverton thought firmly, was for a man or a young boy.

He found it distinctly shocking that a woman, in however wild and primitive a country, should ride astride.

As if she knew what he was thinking Tula gave a little laugh as she said:

'I feel, My Lord, that you are noticing the omission of a pommel, and that I am not dressed for the English hunting-field.'

'What do you know about hunting-fields?' Lord Yelverton asked, to prevent himself from replying to her question.

'Papa has often described to me the conventional life he led in the Shires before he took up archaeology as a pastime, only to find it became an obsession.'

'You would certainly cause a sensation

dressed as you are!' Lord Yelverton said dryly.

'If you feel embarrassed to be with me,' Tula smiled, 'let me assure you that the people around here are used to my appearance, just as they are used to my father. Everything we do is just another stanza in the poems and songs they write about us.'

Lord Yelverton was surprised until he remembered that the Mexicans wrote poems to their gods and sang rather lugubrious chants.

He could imagine Audenshaw, looking as he did and behaving with a disregard of morals that would draw the censure of the women if not the men, would be a perfect subject for the chanting of words whose meaning would dip darkly into the consciousness of the listeners.

He was, however, too anxious to be on his way to stay talking or even arguing with Tula.

Without saying any more he swung

himself into the saddle. They set off and she rode ahead of him.

He could not help noticing that she sat a horse as well as any woman he had ever seen, and that the green silk of her blouse which matched the green of her fringed skirt threw into prominence the gold in her hair.

It was not yet hot enough for her to put on the wide-brimmed straw hat that she had attached to the front of her saddle.

Instead she rode bare-headed and he saw again with surprise that her hair instead of being pinned, as he would have expected, neatly to her head was merely tied with a bow of green ribbon and hung down her back.

'She is as unconventional as her father,' Lord Yelverton told himself and somehow it annoyed him, but he did not understand why.

They rode down the cart-track which led to Ajax Audenshaw's house, crossed the narrow dusty road which led down to the village of Acapulco, and immediately started to climb.

The hills, unlike those through which Lord Yelverton had ridden on his way from Mexico City, were almost bare of vegetation and the rocks had a shining glint to them which told him they contained minerals.

As they climbed and went on climbing the sun became hotter, and after half an hour's riding, Tula brought her horse to a standstill while she took her hat from her saddle and put it on her head.

Lord Yelverton looked back and found he could see the port which the Spanish ships had used and he knew that with its islands for protection against storms there was no more perfect and natural harbour to be found in the whole world.

It was very beautiful with the blue sea breaking on the gold of the beaches and the coconut trees growing down to the edge of the sand.

It struck him that he had found Paradise

and perhaps for the first time, he could understand why Audenshaw was prepared to bury himself in obscurity and be happy, free from the condemnation of society, if it ever found its way to Acapulco.

His thoughts were interrupted by the sound of stones being dislodged and tumbling past him.

He looked round to see that Tula was riding away and he had not realized that she had left him behind.

He followed her quickly, having the strange feeling that if he lost sight of her, he might never find her again.

They rode until it was almost too hot to be endurable. Then high up in the hills they came to a small cluster of houses.

There was no-one to be seen, except a few young children playing in the dust.

Then to Lord Yelverton's surprise Tula, instead of riding on as he had expected, stopped at a small stone hut and dismounted.

'Why are we stopping here?' he asked.

'There is someone with whom you have to speak before we can go any further.'

Lord Yelverton looked at her quizzically.

He had not expected that some sort of permit might be necessary, but that was what Tula's words implied.

Leaving her horse free to crop at the few shrubs that grew between the stones, Tula knocked on the door of the hut and Lord Yelverton heard her speaking in a language he did not understand, to somebody who was inside.

He dismounted wondering if it would be safe to leave his horse free as Tula had left hers, and decided it was unlikely that the animal would wander far.

He then walked to join Tula, but before he could reach her a woman came from the hut and Lord Yelverton knew, though it astonished him, that she was a *Curandera*—a witch.

He had seen them before and on his ride from Mexico City his guides had pointed out a *Curandera* almost every day of their journey.

He knew that to the Mexicans magic was a very important part of their lives, but he had always been told that while witchcraft worked for Mexicans it was well known that foreigners were immune to it.

Then why, Lord Yelverton asked himself angrily, was Tula getting in touch with the village *Curandera?*

He was tempted for the moment to ride on and leave her to follow him.

Then he told himself if she wished to play games and pander to local superstition he would be prepared to tolerate it, if it meant it would help him find the cave.

As he researched very thoroughly any country he visited he was aware that while witchcraft had played an important part in Mexico in ancient times, it was not until the Spanish conquerers came that witchcraft really began to boom.

In the Aztec Empire only those born under the sign of rain were destined by the gods to practise witchcraft; unless one was born to be a witch, there was no chance of becoming one.

But the witches of Spain, Lord Yelverton was aware, deliberately chose to follow that calling. By making a pact with the Devil witches enjoyed the pleasures of the flesh, Satan appeared in the form of a large he-goat and taught them Black Magic.

Most Aztec witches were men. Their hero was the god of Light, the patron of Witches, whose most famous feat was changing himself into a jaguar.

But the witch Tula brought from the dark hovel into the sunlight was not, Lord Yelverton thought, very impressive and he resented having to waste time listening to her, if that was what Tula expected him to do.

Now speaking in Mexican-Spanish which Lord Yelverton could understand, Tula said:

'This is a guest of my father's. He seeks a certain cave which is somewhere in these hills. We need your help, *Curandera,* to find it.'

The *Curandera* looked at Lord Yelverton and he saw that she had cataracts in both of her eyes. Yet her old lined face was turned towards him and he had a feeling that she was looking not at his external appearance, but deep into his soul.

He did not speak, for he had no wish to say anything, and as if Tula was aware of what he was feeling she gave him a glance that he was sure was one of warning.

The *Curandera* went back into her house and returned with a bowl of water.

She sat down on the deep stone which acted as a step and set the bowl down at her side.

Then she held out her hand towards Tula who produced two wild flowers which Lord Yelverton had not noticed she carried before and felt she must have picked them as they walked.

They were quite ordinary wild flowers, and the *Curandera* took them gently in her hand, pulled them petal by petal into pieces and dropped them into the water.

There was silence as she stared at the bowl.

There was no sound and even the children were quiet. Lord Yelverton found he was listening and thought it was not only with his ears but with some inner sense he did not ordinarily use.

The *Curandera* passed her hands over the bowl. Then she said in a strange deep voice that made her sound more like a man than a woman:

'What is being sought is near falling water but there is danger! The soul that guards it is there keeping the vow he made before he died. Beware!'

She raised her head and Lord Yelverton remembered he had not told Tula that he had learned from the seaman that the cave was near water. He wondered if she had read his thoughts.

Tula, who had been sitting on the step while the *Curandera* was staring at the bowl, now rose to her feet.

'Thank you, thank you very much!' she said. 'The *Señor* is also grateful.'

She held out her hand towards Lord Yelverton as she spoke and with a slightly mocking smile he put his hand into his pocket and produced a coin that was the equivalent in English of half-a-sovereign.

He thought Tula might think it was too much, but she took it from him without comment. She did not however give it to the witch, but put it instead on the stone in front of her house.

'May you travel in peace,' the *Curandera* said.

'Your kindness will travel with us,' Tula replied.

The old woman vanished into her cottage leaving the money outside, and Lord Yelverton, grateful that he had to do no more and was not expected to say anything, walked towards his horse.

Tula mounted hers and they rode for some little way before he was able to ride beside her so that he could ask:

'Did you know that the cave was beside water?'

'No. How could I?'

'I thought perhaps you might have read my thoughts.'

'I have tried not to ever since I met you.'

'But last night you felt capable of doing so?'

She did not reply, and after a moment's silence he said:

'I want you to answer my question.'

'Why?' Tula enquired. 'I have found out what you want to know, where the cave is situated.'

'I would have told you if you had asked me.'

There was undoubtedly a mocking smile on her lips as she replied:

'I thought you were testing me.'

Because this was true, there was nothing Lord Yelverton could reply.

After a moment he said in a voice that

held an undoubted note of irritation:

'I dislike superstitions of all sorts, and I do not believe in witches!'

Tula laughed and he thought it was the first time he had heard her laugh spontaneously and joyously as a child might.

Because it was so out of character he looked at her in surprise and she said:

'I am convinced that no Englishman should leave his own tight little island. Papa was just like you when he first came to Mexico. He used to shout aloud as if he would defy the spirits: "I do not believe in you! Go away!" '

'And did they?' Lord Yelverton enquired.

'No, of course not!' Tula answered. 'Mexico is all spirit and there are gods and demons, devils and angels everywhere! And not even the ritual of the Catholic Church could exorcize them!'

'I do not want to believe you,' Lord Yelverton said petulantly as if he was a child.

'It does not matter whether you believe or disbelieve,' Tula said. 'Mexico is the one place in the world where there is no distinction between spirit and matter.'

'What do you mean by that?'

He knew that Tula was thinking before she spoke. Then she said:

'A Mexican does not consider himself as created and therefore external to God. To him everything and everybody is part of creation, a great flood forever flowing in lovely rippling waves.'

Tula spoke with a kind of lilt in her voice that made it hard not to accept what she was saying.

It seemed to Lord Yelverton as if for the moment she conjured up the wonder and fascination of creation shimmering in every leaf and stone, in every thorn and bud.

It was there. It was something he felt he had always known, but it had taken this young girl to put it into words.

The path narrowed and once again Tula was riding ahead of him and he was glad, for he did not want to talk to her; did not want the strange feelings he had felt last night when they were together to be revived.

He just wanted to be himself, his ordinary prosaic self, intent on discovering the history of a long-dead people from some piece of pottery dug out of the earth, from which certain deductions could be made entirely logically without any mystery about it.

Yet he knew as he followed Tula that he felt as if he was riding through a thick mist: that he would not find a land that was familiar and expected as the mist lifted, but instead a strange, exotic dream-world that had substance only in the awakening of his mind to possibilities he had never acknowledged before.

They rode for perhaps a quarter of an hour and now they were high up on the hills. After twisting round a great boulder the path turned inward and Lord Yelverton saw there was a deep valley ahead.

The rocks were sharp and barren of any vegetation, and as they turned again the path was so narrow that he was afraid of his horse slipping and throwing him from the saddle.

Then Lord Yelverton heard a strange sound.

It was like the roar of sea-waves and a moment later he saw what was causing it.

Ahead was a cascade of water gleaming in the sunshine and magnificent in the rush of its fall down into a pool before it flowed away through the rocks, gradually moving more slowly until it finally vanished into the valley.

It came to Lord Yelverton's mind that this was where the *Curandera* had said he would find the cave, and it was also obvious that this was the cascade to which the seaman had referred.

He tried to find some explanation as to why the witch with her eyes almost blind, should have told him where to go, but he could only fall back on the feeble explanation that either she or Tula could read his thoughts.

Whatever the explanation, he was here and as he looked at the rocks on each side of the cascade he thought it should not be hard to locate the cave, unless of course, it was on the other side of the valley.

As there was no possibility of the horses going any further, he dismounted and Tula did the same.

Then because it was impossible to hear anything that was said unless they were close to each other, he moved nearer to her to ask:

'Where do you think the cave is likely to be?'

Lord Yelverton spoke casually as if it was not of particular importance and she answered him in the same way:

'I have no idea. We shall just have to guess.'

'What I propose,' Lord Yelverton said, 'is that I climb up first to the top of the torrent and if I find anything of significance you can come and join me.'

He thought as he spoke there was a faint smile on her lips and that she was sure his reason for going first was that he wanted the excitement of finding the cave and had no wish to share it with her.

Actually he had thought it unnecessary for them both to exert themselves on what would be a steep, rather rough climb over the stones.

But if that was what she wanted to think he was not particularly concerned and he knew without her saying so, that she was half-hoping he would be disappointed and would find nothing.

'Wait here!' he said sharply making it a command.

Tula took off her hat and sat down on a smooth-surfaced boulder, her eyes not on Lord Yelverton but on the torrent where the spray catching the sunlight created a rainbow which stretched from the top to the bottom of it.

The horses had their heads down

cropping what little they could find, and
Lord Yelverton thought the torrent was
such a beautiful sight that they might in
fact, be two tourists merely sight-seeing.

He had an unaccountable feeling that
Tula should be wishing him luck, instead
of which she did not even look at him as
he left her.

As he had anticipated, it was quite a
difficult climb over the sharp uneven rocks.
His feet kept slipping and the sharp edges
of the rocks hurt his hands.

He was however, used to climbing and
he did not find it particularly arduous.

It took him a little over three minutes
to approach the top, where he saw below
the sky-line there were inserted deep into
the rocks two or three dark openings to
little caves.

Lord Yelverton felt his heart leap.

He had found what he was seeking, and
he thought now that even without Tula's
help he would somehow have found his
way here.

It was almost as if the two precious objects he carried in his trouser pocket had guided him back to their home.

He had been conscious of them all the time they were riding, just as he had been conscious of them ever since they had come into his possession.

Then he thought that when he reached the caves he could almost trust them to show him which was the one he sought, where for three hundred years they had lain in safety, before they had been stolen away.

Lord Yelverton hauled himself up onto a ledge on the rock which was just in front of the caves.

It was wider than he had expected, at least three feet, and led on to the edge of the cascade, almost like a path.

He put his leg over the edge of it; hauled himself up and was on his feet facing the caves that he had seen from below.

He was aware now that two of the openings were very shallow, but the third, which was dark and dusty, obviously extended far into the rock and he was sure this was the place he sought and where the treasure lay.

It was a moment of triumph.

Then as he stood looking at the caves he realized that he had come without the equipment that was necessary if as he expected, he would have to dig away the accumulation of dust and stones before he could proceed into what he suspected was a hidden chamber far down in the rock.

'Tomorrow,' he told himself, 'I will bring my men, and we will start work.'

He felt elated and excited at the idea, but he told himself it was only right and polite that he should show the cave to Tula because she had brought him here.

He turned round to beckon her to climb up and join him but to his surprise she was not looking at him and watching, as he had thought she would, his progress to the top, but was staring at the cascade.

It was a moment before he could attract her attention.

Then at last, perhaps because he was willing her to do so, she looked towards him and he waved his hand.

Even as he did so, something very strange happened.

He felt himself being propelled—there was no other word for it—away from the cave and along the ledge.

He tried to resist what seemed like the power of a great wind or a strange force which almost swept him off his feet so that it was impossible to keep his balance.

He struggled, but it was useless.

Then with a feeling of sheer horror he found himself at the edge of the swift flowing torrent.

Desperately, frantically he struggled, but to no avail.

He felt himself falling forward and downwards, until as he struck the water everything went dark.

4

Tula saw Lord Yelverton fall into the cascade and jumped to her feet with a cry of horror.

Then she held her breath as she watched his body hurtling down the foaming water into the pool.

He was whirled around, then out onto the fall at the end of it where the waves rose and fell until finally they subsided into a swift current winding between green banks sprinkled with water hyacinths.

It was then she started to run, stumbling over the rocks and boulders, slipping and once or twice falling on her knees, before finally she was level with Lord Yelverton who was now floating face downwards, his arms outstretched which kept him on the surface.

He was still being carried downstream but by no means swiftly, and she was wondering how she could reach him when two men appeared.

They were Mexicans and one of them she recognized, an older man with greying hair.

'Diaz!' she exclaimed, and it was a cry of relief.

He did not answer her but gave a sharp word of command to the younger man and they waded into the stream up to their waists.

But they could not reach Lord Yelverton and he floated away from them.

They tried again a little lower down, and this time Diaz held the younger man by one hand as he waded further out, until the water was up to his arm-pits.

Then with his other hand outstretched he managed to catch hold of Lord Yelverton.

It was only a question of time before they pulled him to the side and between them lifted him onto the bank.

They laid him on the grass face downwards and sitting astride his prostrate body Diaz began to manipulate him in an effort to expel the water he had swallowed and bring him back to consciousness.

As Tula watched anxiously he turned Lord Yelverton over onto his back.

He was very pale and his eyes were closed and with a feeling of horror Tula felt that he looked as if he was carved in marble and already lying on a tomb.

In a voice that was hardly audible and did not sound like her own, she asked:

'Is he...dead?'

Diaz looked at her and replied:

'He does not breathe.'

Tula went down on her knees and undid the buttons of Lord Yelverton's wet shirt to lay her hand on his heart.

She could feel nothing.

She looked up at Diaz who stood beside her.

'How can we save him?'

He did not reply for a moment and she said insistently:

'You must...know what to...do. Quetzalcoatl is the god of life.'

There was a faint smile on Diaz's lips which she did not understand as he replied:

'You must make him breathe.'

'How? How?' Tula questioned.

Her fingers moved over Lord Yelverton's heart as if she was trying to make it beat.

Then Diaz said quietly:

'It is breath he wants and that you can give him.'

For a moment Tula stared at him not comprehending what he was trying to say.

'The kiss of life,' Diaz said, as if she had asked the question.

It was then she understood and she bent forward and put her lips against Lord Yelverton's.

Forcing them slightly open she blew her own breath into his mouth feeling as she did so that Quetzalcoatl had told her what to do.

She could feel the life-force flowing through her body, out through her lips and into Lord Yelverton.

Her hand was still on his heart, when suddenly she felt there was a faint response beneath his cold skin and yet she could not be sure.

She went on breathing, praying, thinking of how she had said to Lord Yelverton that everything and everybody in Mexico was part of creation, a great flood forever flowing in lovely rippling waves.

It was that creative force which she was giving him now, making it flow from her body into his and she knew quite simply that she was giving him life.

Now there was no mistaking that Lord Yelverton's heart was beating.

She raised her head and looked up again at Diaz.

'He lives!'

There was a note of awe in her voice.

'He lives,' Diaz confirmed.

Lord Yelverton felt as if he was coming back through a long dark tunnel to where there was a faint point of light that grew larger and larger until the darkness vanished and he opened his eyes.

He was conscious of a feeling as if he was one cast aching bruise from his head to his toes and every part of his body was painful, but at the same time, as if after a long dream his brain was clearing.

For a moment he could not think where he was.

Then as he saw the canvas of a tent above him, he thought he must be on his way to Acapulco, sleeping outside some small hamlet or amongst the wooded hills over which he was travelling.

Then someone came and knelt down beside him and he saw it was Tula.

As her eyes looked into his he remembered.

He had reached the end of his journey,

he had met Audenshaw and he had found the cave.

Then he recalled falling into the cascade. 'What—happened?' he tried to ask.

His voice was merely a hoarse croak and Tula put her hand behind his neck and lifted his head very gently as she held a glass to his lips.

It tasted of fruit juice and was as delicious as the drink which Ajax Audenshaw had given him the night he arrived when he was so thirsty.

Now he could remember everything: Tula's reluctance to take him to the cave, the *Curandera* who warned him of the danger, and the terrifying moment when he had felt himself propelled by some unseen and unexplained force to the edge of the cascade.

Tula had taken the glass from his lips and put his head back again onto the pillow.

'Go to sleep,' she said.

He would have expostulated because

there was so much he wanted to know, then he felt her fingers massaging his forehead very gently and mesmerically.

He wanted to talk to her, but instead he found the rhythmic movements of her fingers hypnotic and he could think of nothing but them as he fell asleep...

★ ★ ★ ★

When Lord Yelverton woke again he realized it was night and there was a lantern beside him on the ground.

For a moment he thought he was alone, then he saw that just inside the flap of the tent which was open to the night there was a man.

Although he was sitting in the shadows Lord Yelverton knew he was a Mexican, that he was elderly and had a proud bearing, or perhaps he merely sensed that he was not an ordinary peasant.

He had been looking up at the stars when Lord Yelverton first saw him.

Now almost as if the man felt that he called him he rose and came into the tent to crouch down beside Lord Yelverton as he lay on his travelling-mattress on the ground.

'You would like a drink, *Señor?*'

The Mexican addressed him in the words of a servant, and yet somehow Lord Yelverton knew he spoke to him as an equal.

'Who—are you?'

'I am Diaz. I am looking after you while the *Señorita* Tula sleeps.'

'She has been nursing me?'

It was a question to which Lord Yelverton already knew the answer.

'She saved your life!'

There was a pause. Then Lord Yelverton said:

'I cannot think how it happened—but I fell into the cascade. How did the *Señorita* prevent me from drowning?'

'You had drowned! No-one has ever fallen from the Cascade and lived!'

'Then how did the *Señorita*—save me?'

'The *Señorita* will tell you that herself,' Diaz replied. 'Now you must sleep. You are lucky you have no bones broken.'

Lord Yelverton wanted to ask how he knew that for certain and if he was a doctor, but it was too much effort and sleep enveloped him again as if he was held in the arms of the goddess of the earth.

★ ★ ★ ★

Lord Yelverton heard the sound of Tula's laughter above the music of the cascade.

He knew now that the sound of the water which had been with him when he slept, woke and slept again, had soothed him and made him in a strange manner, feel as if he was loved and protected.

Now Tula was laughing and it was like the song of the birds when the sun rose.

She came into the tent.

While Lord Yelverton had slept one side

132

had been opened. Behind her he could see the green of the opposite bank of the stream and realized that the first rays of the sun were like specks of gold upon the shrubs and flowers.

For a moment Tula's figure blotted everything else from his sight, then he saw that she carried a bunch of flowers in her hand and their colours of crimson and yellow seemed to light the tent.

'Diaz tells me you had a good night,' Tula said, 'and you will therefore feel hungry and want breakfast. Jiminez is cooking it for you.'

She put the flowers down on the blanket with which he was covered, then before he could ask any questions she moved away while Diaz came to make him comfortable and place more pillows behind his head.

He also washed and shaved him and by the time Tula returned with a very appetizing breakfast Lord Yelverton felt more like himself.

He was still aware that almost every part

of his body was very painful which came from the buffeting he must have endured while he was unconscious in the rough waters of the cascade.

He knew that it was in fact, a miracle that he had been able to survive such an experience.

He wanted to talk about it to Tula who he knew had been the only person who had witnessed exactly what had happened.

But first there was a trout from the stream to eat, besides eggs that were small but very satisfying, and coffee that he knew was grown in many parts of Mexico.

Only when the meal was finished and Jiminez had come to take away the tray, did Lord Yelverton say with a slight smile:

'I see we have set up house here.'

Tula had been sitting just outside the open side of the tent and the sun coming through the trees above them turned her hair to gold.

'It was impossible to move you.'

'I can understand that,' Lord Yelverton replied. 'Diaz has told me that no-one has fallen down the cascade as I did, and lived.'

He paused for a moment before he asked:

'Why?'

There was a few moments' silence before Tula said:

'I feel there are many questions which you will want to ask, but there is no hurry for you to know the answers and you still need rest.'

'I am feeling stronger this morning, and almost my old self,' Lord Yelverton replied, 'and as you can imagine, my curiosity will prevent me from resting as you wish me to do, unless you will answer my questions.'

'Very well,' Tula conceded. 'What comes first?'

Lord Yelverton thought for a moment. Then he said:

'You saw me fall. How did it happen?'

He had a feeling as he spoke that she had been wondering how she should answer him, and she parried it by saying:

'Only you can explain that.'

'I wish I could explain it. All I can say is some wind, a force, anything you like to call it, pushed me from the ledge into the torrent.'

He had started by speaking calmly, but now his voice grew angry at the thought of how impossible it had been for him to save himself.

He felt he had been weak and ineffectual to be overwhelmed by a superior strength to his own, but he knew there had been nothing at the time that he could do about it.

'How can it have happened?' he asked now, and his tone was sharp.

'What is the point of my telling you what you already know?' Tula asked.

'Was that the reason why you tried to prevent me from coming here in search of the treasure?' Lord Yelverton asked.

136

'The *Curandera* told you it might be dangerous.'

'Magic! Superstition! How can you expect me to believe in such nonsense?' Lord Yelverton demanded.

Tula gave a little laugh, and it seemed part of the sunshine that enveloped her.

'You do not *have* to believe anything.'

'I want an explanation.'

'From whom?'

'Damn it all!' Lord Yelverton said. 'You cannot really seriously expect me to believe that the spirit of some wretched man who was sacrificed hundreds of years ago is still there to prevent people like myself from approaching what he had been told to guard?'

Tula made an expressive gesture with her hands.

'You can prove whether it is true quite easily.'

'How?'

'By trying as soon as you are well enough to enter the cave once again.'

There was silence for a moment. Then it was Lord Yelverton's turn to laugh.

'*Touché!* You know as well as I do I am not going to risk being drowned or smashed to pieces for a second time.'

'Very well then,' Tula said. 'There is nothing you can do, but accept that in Mexico superstitions are based on truth.'

Lord Yelverton was silent.

He was trying to persuade himself that there was a whirlwind at that particular point in the rock, or a passage of air of such unexpected strength that it was like a gale.

He knew none of these explanations would hold water and there only remained the indisputable fact that he had been propelled from the front of the cave and thrown into the cascade in which he should, by all the laws of nature, have lost his life.

He realized while he was thinking it out that Tula was looking at him with a faint smile on her lips and a twinkle in her eyes.

It was an expression he had not seen before and it suddenly struck him that her attitude towards him seemed to have changed.

She was no longer aloof or apart and hating him as an intruder, but in nursing him back to health had accepted him.

What this acceptance meant Lord Yelverton had yet to find out.

'Now we come to the next question,' he said. 'I can guess that Diaz and Jiminez pulled me out of the stream but by then I must have been drowned. How did you bring me back to life?'

Tula turned her head away from him and all he could see was her profile with her straight little nose and her firm chin, as he had seen it that first evening when she had been looking at the stars.

She did not reply and after a moment he said:

'I am waiting, Tula.'

'Diaz will tell you.'

'He told me to ask you.'

She gave him a quick glance.

Again there was silence. Then Lord Yelverton said:

'I want to know.'

'Why?'

'Because it is something which happened to me, and I am alive instead of being dead. Surely you would expect me to be curious about this as well as about the guardian of the cave?'

Once again Tula was smiling as she said quickly:

'So you accept that there is a guardian?'

'I can hardly expect you to have missed that admission on my part,' Lord Yelverton said ruefully.

'Like Papa you are beginning to understand that Mexico is different.'

'Very different!' Lord Yelverton agreed.

Then as if he felt that Tula was evading his other question he said:

'Tell me what I want to know. How did you save me?'

He knew perceptively that there was

something about it she was unwilling to tell him, and yet he knew it was the reason that he was alive, and not dead, and that he could never rest until he knew the truth.

Now she turned her head away from him again and after a moment said in a low voice:

'Diaz told me what to do.'

'Why should he know?'

'He has knowledge of certain things which are not known to everybody.'

'I think what you are hiding from me,' Lord Yelverton said slowly, 'is that he is a follower of Quetzalcoatl.'

He knew as he spoke that once again he was so attuned to her, as he had been before, that he could read her thoughts.

That she did not deny what he said but appeared to accept it, he thought was the inevitable response, almost as if they had been leading up to it like two actors in a play.

'So like you,' Lord Yelverton said very

quietly, 'Diaz follows the Plumed Serpent, the symbol of the mysterious forces of the earth.'

Again Tula did not speak, but he knew she accepted what he had said.

'What did he tell you to do? Or rather,' Lord Yelverton added, 'how did he tell you to use this mysterious force?'

He was feeling not for words but for understanding, and because he was intrigued and vitally interested he felt almost as if he was fighting to make Tula tell him what he wished to hear.

'I know I am right,' he said and his voice rose. 'You and Diaz knew how to save me because somehow you harnessed the force in which you both believe, which comes from Quetzalcoatl and used it on me. What did you do?'

There was a command in his tone as he asked the question, and as if Tula had to answer him, she turned to look at him and he felt there was an expression in her eyes that was almost mystical.

For a moment they looked at each other. Then Lord Yelverton knew that although she wished to look away from him she was unable to do so.

'Tell me,' he said softly.

'I...gave you...life when your heart... stopped beating.'

'How?'

'I...breathed it from my...body into yours.'

As she spoke the colour rose in her pale cheeks and Lord Yelverton knew how she had done it.

'The kiss of life!' he said very quietly.

He thought that far back in the past, perhaps even in another life, he had heard the expression.

Tula's cheeks were suffused with colour and she rose from where she was sitting and walked away to stand on the edge of the stream looking down into the flowing water which was so clear that she could see small fish moving over the rocky bottom.

Lord Yelverton thought she seemed to fit into the landscape as if she was an indivisible part of it and no longer a separate entity.

Once again he thought of her belief in being part of creation and not created or external to God.

He felt this was a secret he had certainly discovered for himself and he thought that not only was it true, but he was in fact a part of Tula and she of him because she had breathed life into his body when he had already died.

It was almost impossible to understand, and yet it had happened.

Through Tula he was living, able to talk to her and be with her but for the instructions which she had received from Diaz he would by now have been buried in this obscure part of Mexico and quickly forgotten.

He wondered what he could say or how he could express his gratitude.

Then, because he realized it was difficult

to talk to anyone who had her back to him, he called:

'Tula, come here! I want you!'

She turned in unexpected obedience and came through the opening of the tent.

Lord Yelverton put out his hand.

'You have to help me.'

'What is the matter? Are you in pain?'

'I am tired, not in my body but in my mind. I am bewildered, and perhaps a little frightened. I had no idea until now of how much there is to know of which I am completely ignorant.'

He saw her eyes light up at his words. Then almost as if he compelled her, she moved towards him and took his outstretched hand.

'You must not do too much too quickly,' she said. 'Diaz is insistent that you need rest and quiet.'

Lord Yelverton's fingers closed over hers and he drew her closer until she sat down on the ground beside him.

He still held her hand and he felt she

would like to escape from him but was not certain how she could do so without hurting his feelings.

Then as if he could read the thoughts that passed through her mind, he said:

'You must realize I have capitulated, unconditionally surrendered if you like, and it is considered chivalrous to treat a fallen enemy with kindness.'

Tula smiled.

'I think I am a little suspicious of such humility, but I will tell you what you wish to know. Where shall we start?'

'With Diaz,' Lord Yelverton said. 'Who is he?'

'He is a very intelligent man, and has had a certain amount of education.'

'Go on!'

'He is a Priest, if that is the right word, of the cult of Quetzalcoatl which exists in many parts of Mexico and has a small but faithful following here in Acapulco.'

Lord Yelverton remembered that Quetzalcoatl had been a Priest-King.

In descriptions of him he had been credited with being both the Divine Feathered Serpent and the last Priest-King of Tula, leader of the highest priestly party.

Now he could understand why Tula with her particular name had been drawn to a cult which had only been vaguely mentioned as still existing in the books he had read about Mexico.

He thought that he could understand her finding such a particular deity attractive, because it was Quetzalcoatl who in becoming the god of the Morning Star had denounced human sacrifice and in the Toltec golden age only snakes and butterflies were sacrificed.

All civil wars led to the movement of people and the war in Tula between the kindly Quetzalcoatl and his complete opposite in the person of Tezcatlipica dispersed refugees all over Mexico.

Lord Yelverton could understand that wherever they went there were still those who worshipped Quetzalcoatl, believing that one day he would return to gather them together in the quiet, peace and happiness that had once been theirs.

'So Diaz through his priestly office knew how to save my life,' he said reflectively.

'He is a good man.'

'I am prepared to accept that. But will you help me?'

'In what way?'

'You know quite well that my head is bloody but not bowed. I cannot give up my quest.'

Tula gave a little cry.

Now instead of trying to escape from the fingers that held hers she seemed to cling to him.

'You cannot be so mad, so crazy as to risk death for a second time!'

'I am prepared to do so,' Lord Yelverton said, 'but I think I should not be handicapped by being weaponless.'

He saw that Tula did not understand, and said with a smile that was only slightly mocking:

'If the spirit that guards the treasure is a follower of Quetzalcoatl, then I must approach him not as a foe, but as a friend.'

Tula turned to stare at him incredulously.

'Are you saying that you are planning to pretend to believe in Quetzalcoatl in order to obtain access to the cave?'

Lord Yelverton looked at her.

'You know as well as I do that the forces we are dealing with would not be deceived by pretence or imitation of the real thing.'

'Then what are you...saying?'

'I am saying quite simply, that I now accept what is for you an entirely reasonable explanation of my being hurled into the torrent.'

'I do not believe you...'

'It is true,' he said. 'Even with my logical, prosaic mind I can find no other possible explanation as to how a man of my strength and stamina should have been propelled as easily as if I was a leaf or a twig, into the cascade.'

'You believe that?' Tula asked incredulously.

'I believe because I have no choice,' Lord Yelverton answered. 'Taking that as our foundation we will start from there. Talk to Diaz. Ask him to help me and assure him that I am not wishing to acquire either personal possessions or fame.'

He paused for a moment, to say seriously:

'If as you think, the things hidden in the cave will tell us more about Quetzalcoatl than is known already, it will not only be of absorbing interest to the archaeological world, but an inestimable help to people like yourself and Diaz who obviously are anxious to know more about the god they worship.'

Tula had looked at Lord Yelverton with wide eyes all the time he was speaking, and now she reached forward to place her free hand on top of his which still held her other hand in his grasp.

'You mean that...really and truly?' she asked.

'I believe it,' he said quietly. 'I have fought against it, tried to laugh at myself, but now after being nearly drowned you have convinced me.'

'I cannot believe you...and yet I want to.'

'I am only admitting that there is something strange and abnormal and definitely supernatural about what happened to me,' Lord Yelverton said, 'but you and Diaz can take it from there and at least I consent to be your pupil.'

Tula's eyes were searching his face as if she wanted to be sure, completely sure, that he was telling her the truth and not just pandering to her in order to get his own way.

As if he felt that his fate still hung in the balance Lord Yelverton said quietly:

'Surely you realize that if you saved me from dying I must have been worth saving?

And perhaps the gods, whoever they may be, intended that I should live.'

He saw her whole face light up as if she accepted what he said. Then she jumped to her feet and ran swiftly from the tent.

She disappeared from his sight, but he could hear her voice ringing out as she called:

'Diaz! Diaz!'

It seemed to Lord Yelverton as if it was the song of the birds, the voice of spring, and the music that came from the cascade.

★ ★ ★ ★

'You will have to wait for at least another twenty-four hours, *Señor.*'

Diaz was massaging Lord Yelverton with an oil that smelt of flowers and which he had already learned had certain herbs in it, that had the property of healing.

Whether it was the oil or the massage, or perhaps some magic quality in his hands,

Lord Yelverton felt that every time Diaz treated him the bruises and the pain of them began to recede from his body and he felt immeasurably stronger.

While Diaz worked he would not talk, explaining that he had to concentrate on what he was doing.

This meant, Lord Yelverton knew, that he tried to pour the life-force through his fingers to heal, renew and invigorate.

To Lord Yelverton the last four days had been very strange ones.

Since he had come back to consciousness and talked to Tula, he found they were camping beneath the trees by the stream and he felt he was isolated in a world that belonged not to mortal beings but to the gods.

Only someone as eccentric as Audenshaw, he knew, would have been content to let his daughter stay with him under the circumstances without thinking it might damage her reputation, or cause a scandal.

However when he thought about it, Lord

Yelverton was sure that there were few people in Acapulco to be scandalized by anything that Audenshaw or his family did and everything that could be said about them had been said already.

Nevertheless he found it strange that anyone so beautiful as Tula should be left so free by an English father, whatever his own morals might be.

And yet he knew that no chaperon could be more effective than Tula's purity and complete lack of self-consciousness where being a woman was concerned.

It had never struck her, he knew, that when nursing and ministering to him he was an attractive man whom she should try to attract or might flirt with him.

Instead he was her patient and therefore impersonal.

If she was sometimes a little shy of him as a man, it was rather because of their beliefs being at variance than her physical awareness that they were of different sexes.

It was to Diaz that she looked with an expression in her blue eyes of reverence, and she accepted what he said to her as if he was in fact, a priest ordained in Holy Orders.

That, Lord Yelverton was certain, was what she did feel about the elderly man and he himself found Diaz an interesting and complex character, and very different from the Mexicans he had known in the past.

Although he plied him with questions about the cult of Quetzalcoatl and his beliefs in the God-Priest, Diaz would tell him very little.

'Now that you are interested, *Señor,* you will find out for yourself,' he said. 'You seek Quetzalcoatl with your mind. What you have to do now is to find him with your spirit, or what the Christians call their soul.'

'And if I cannot do so?'

'If you seek you will find.'

This was the reply Diaz gave many

times to questions which he did not wish to answer because, as Lord Yelverton understood, it was for each man to find for himself what it was necessary for him to know.

After having studied many ancient people and read dozens of books on them it was almost uncanny, Lord Yelverton thought, to find he was developing a new appreciation of everything he had learnt in the past.

It was not only what Diaz and Tula had told him, it was as if they all three of them communicated without words, and he could learn too from the sound of the cascade, the song of the birds and the buzz of the bees hovering over the flowers.

They were all part of a creative force and he himself merged with them and in that merging there was no need for it to be translated into words.

'Can I get up tomorrow?' Lord Yelverton asked Diaz.

'The muscles of your legs are still weak,

Señor,' Diaz replied. 'You have exercised them while lying on your back, and that is good. But if you wish to walk a little on the level ground it will do you no harm. But it must be several days yet before you climb the rocks to the cave.'

'You know that is what I intend to do?' Lord Yelverton asked.

'I know it is what you will do.'

'What will happen?'

Diaz made a movement of his shoulders that was very explicit.

'I have no wish to risk being drowned for a second time,' Lord Yelverton said.

'Then do not attempt what may be dangerous.'

Lord Yelverton smiled.

'If I tamely packed up and went home, I can imagine how both you and Tula would despise me.'

Without Diaz agreeing he knew that was true and after a moment the older man said:

'There is one way in which you can be

safe, but you may not like to hear it.'

'Why should you say that? You know I have to see what is in the cave, and as I told both you and Tula I am certain that what I shall find there will be of interest and of great importance to all the people who worship Quetzalcoatl.'

'I accept that,' Diaz replied. 'At the same time I am afraid. The guardian of the cave has already shown his strength. I know that your intentions are for the best, but who knows if he will agree?'

'You said there was a way I could be safe,' Lord Yelverton said. 'What is it?'

As he spoke a voice from outside the tent asked:

'Can I come in?'

'One moment,' Lord Yelverton replied.

Diaz had finished massaging him and pulled the blankets over the lower part of his body, but his chest was bare and now Diaz helped him into his pyjama coat which his servants had brought with the tents and his personal belongings from Audenshaw's house.

They had been sent home because as Tula explained there was not room for them and there was really nothing for them to do.

Lord Yelverton accepted her explanation, but he thought too she had wanted Diaz and herself to nurse him without interference, and he knew that his man-servant would be extremely jealous at what he considered his rightful position being usurped.

Now Lord Yelverton buttoned his pyjama coat and said:

'You may come in.'

Tula appeared round the side of the tent.

'I came to ask you what you would like for luncheon. Jiminez has brought us a young chicken and also several lobsters but it is up to you which you prefer.'

'Before I decide on such an important question,' Lord Yelverton answered, 'Diaz has something to say and I wish you to listen to him.'

'What is it?' Tula asked coming further into the tent.

She sat down at the end of Lord Yelverton's bed and looked at Diaz who was beside him rubbing his hands clean of the healing oil he had used.

Diaz did not reply and after a moment Lord Yelverton said:

'Diaz has told me he knows a way in which I might enter the cave and be completely safe. He is not yet certain the guardian will accept me as a convert.'

There was a faint smile on his lips as he said the last words and Tula smiled at him in response. Then she said to Diaz:

'Have you really thought of a way of how His Lordship can be safe? I am afraid, so desperately afraid, that he might be hurled into the cascade for a second time.'

There was silence, and both Lord Yelverton and Tula waited. Then Diaz said slowly in his deep voice that sometimes seemed as if he was inspired in what he said:

'There is one way in which the *Señor* would be safe and protected, as you would be yourself.'

'What is that?'

'Because you are a child of Quetzalcoatl,' Diaz said, 'because the guardian of the cave would know this, then if the *Señor* approached at your side not just as an explorer as he is, but as your husband with you as his wife, then Quetzalcoatl will ensure his safety.'

5

There was a stupefied silence while both Lord Yelverton and Tula stared at Diaz as if he had exploded a bomb between them.

Then Tula with a catch in her breath said:

'No...no...of course...not!'

Because she had said the words that had been on Lord Yelverton's lips, it made him almost instinctively take the opposite view.

'It is certainly an idea,' he said slowly.

'I have no other solution to your problem,' Diaz said simply, 'but I understand the *Señorita's* reluctance and yours *Señor.*'

He would have risen to his feet but Lord Yelverton put out his hand to stop him.

'One moment, Diaz,' he said, 'let us think this over carefully. I think I can understand why you say if I accept your suggestion the guardian of the cave as a follower of Quetzalcoatl will accept it too.'

'You cannot be sure of that,' Tula said quickly.

Lord Yelverton looked at her first with an expression of surprise in his eyes, then as he realized why she was prevaricating there was a definite twinkle in them, as he said:

'I think that should be my line, not yours.'

'I am well aware, My Lord, that you feel this is carrying play-acting too far,' Tula said defiantly.

'Who is speaking of play-acting?' Lord Yelverton asked. 'I have already told you in all sincerity that I know that I was thrown into the cascade by some supernatural, uncanny force for which there is no explanation.'

He looked at Diaz as he went on:

'You tell me it is because the cave contains relics of Quetzalcoatl. Very well, I accept that it is a follower of his religion who is defending them.'

There was silence as he finished speaking. Then he said, speaking to Diaz:

'Make your arrangements for Tula and me to be married and afterwards we will all approach the cave with confidence.'

Tula drew in her breath to protest.

Then she saw from the expression on Diaz's face that he was pleased that his suggestion had been accepted and also that Lord Yelverton had invited him to enter the cave together with them.

There were a great many things she wanted to say, but feeling she would be overruled both by Diaz and by Lord Yelverton, she bit back the words even as they came to her lips.

Diaz rose to say quietly:

'I will arrange to marry you, *Señor* and *Señorita*, the day after tomorrow, but only if the *Señor* is well enough.'

'I shall be well enough,' Lord Yelverton said positively.

Diaz went from the tent and Lord Yelverton smiled at Tula who was still sitting on the end of his bed.

'Do not look so upset,' he pleaded. 'It is not very complimentary!'

'I do not wish to do...this,' she said in a low voice.

'Why not?'

'I feel it is a...mockery.'

'On your part, or on mine?'

'You know you do not really believe in Quetzalcoatl.'

'I have already told you I accept, because it is quite logical, that the power which tried to destroy me has come connection with the cave which contains objects used in the worship of one particular god. I am not so unimaginative or so obtuse that I cannot accept such things when the evidence is apparent.'

He spoke firmly and he felt that Tula

was impressed; at the same time, she looked anxious.

Then she said:

'It will not be, of course, a...a legal marriage.'

'No, of course not,' Lord Yelverton answered, 'and it is certainly one that could not take place anywhere else except in Mexico.'

Tula looked relieved. Then she rose to her feet.

'I will go and tell Jiminez,' she said in a different voice, 'to cook a lobster for your luncheon.'

She went before Lord Yelverton had a chance to say any more.

When he was alone he lay back against his pillows looking at the greenery in the sunlight outside and thought it would be impossible to make anyone in England believe this was really happening.

'What does it matter?' he asked himself, 'whether I am married by a priest who has no standing except in his own faith, to a girl whom, once I have left Acapulco, I shall never see again?'

He thought with a smile of amusement it was something that one day when he was too old to go exploring he might incorporate in his memoirs.

Certainly Audenshaw and his strange household would warrant a page or two if only as a light relief from the more serious descriptions of explorations he had undertaken.

When he was in Egypt he had written various articles for the Geographical Society, not as many as they wanted from him, but at least two or three that described his findings and the way they increased our knowledge of the history of the Pharaohs.

But he knew that what had happened to him since he arrived in Acapulco would not be considered by the Geographical Society as suitable material for their readers, especially Ajax Audenshaw's love-life.

For the first time since he had been injured Lord Yelverton wondered how

Audenshaw's household were managing without Tula.

She did not come back to him until an aroma from the open fire over which Jiminez was cooking told Lord Yelverton that his luncheon was nearly ready.

Then she brought him one of the long cool fruit drinks that he enjoyed and he liked the way she varied them with different fruits from day to day.

When he took it from her and thanked her, he said:

'I have been wondering since you are here nursing me so kindly and effectively what is happening to all those children. Without anyone to keep them in order your father must find them an irritating distraction from his painting.'

'They are quite all right.'

'Who is looking after them?' Lord Yelverton persisted.

'One of the teachers who instructs Lucette. She is Bavarian and a very capable woman of over forty.'

'She needs to be capable in such circumstances,' Lord Yelverton said dryly.

'The children love her and even Papa finds, because she is intelligent, that when she is there he does not miss me.'

'I am glad I am not depriving him of his peace of mind, if nothing else.'

'Papa always does what he wants to do, and if he wished me to return he would insist on it.'

'And you would obey him?'

'Of course.'

Lord Yelverton took a sip of his drink before he said:

'What is going to happen to you in the future, Tula? You can hardly go on living for the next twenty years in such a strange, slightly reprehensible household. The children will grow up and where will you go when your father dies?'

Tula looked startled.

'There is no chance of that.'

'There is always a chance that we will lose our lives one way or another, just as I might have lost mine a few days ago, and I am much younger than your father.'

Lord Yelverton knew his words surprised and in a way upset her, and because it was something he had no wish to do, he said:

'I am not anticipating your father's death. What I am really trying to say is that you are very beautiful and should be living a very different sort of life and one where you have a chance of finding a husband.'

'I have no wish to be married,' Tula said quickly.

Lord Yelverton laughed.

'That was very obvious when Diaz suggested it!'

He thought she might explain that was not what she had been talking about and Lord Yelverton said:

'I am only teasing! The sort of marriage I am really talking about, is a proper marriage to a man who will look after you and give you a home of your own.'

Tula turned to leave the tent and when she was actually outside in the sunshine she looked back to say:

'There is no need, My Lord, for you to concern yourself with my future. When you find what you seek in the cave there will be nothing to keep you any longer in Acapulco!'

She walked away and Lord Yelverton chuckled to himself as he thought:

'I have been snubbed very effectively for trying to interfere.'

At the same time because Tula was so lovely and intelligent it seemed to him a waste that she should be isolated in a place so far off the beaten track that he was quite certain she might go for years more without ever meeting an eligible suitor.

He supposed he could understand why in her loneliness, with a father who was always engaged in amatory adventures with women, she had turned to the cult of Quetzalcoatl.

It was like women all over the world

who, when there was no sexual interest in their lives, found a consolation in religion.

Whatever happiness the worship of a long-dead god might give her, Lord Yelverton still thought it was a waste of her youth.

He knew she was right in saying that as soon as he found what was in the cave he would leave Acapulco and Mexico.

He had never intended to stay very long and he had, in fact, promised his relatives that after his trip to Egypt he would spend at least a year in England seeing to the Yelverton estate and the great house that had been the home of his ancestors for five hundred years.

There were a great many things that needed his attention there besides the fact that he had to catalogue and get ready for an exhibition the last findings he had sent home from Egypt.

It was only the jaguar bone and the amber which the seaman had offered him which had made him change his mind and leave for Mexico almost immediately after he reached England.

Now, he told himself, he would make amends by staying for the next few years at home before he set out on any further journey of exploration.

'This one has certainly been worthwhile,' he told himself and was again wondering how much was hidden in the cave.

If the jaguar bone and the amber were anything to go by, the discovery of so much from the days of Tula's grandeur would add enormously to the very sparse knowledge, of the region where the Toltec Chieftain had established his Kingdom.

'I have been amazingly lucky,' Lord Yelverton thought, 'and it is Tula who has made it possible for me to find the treasure for which most archaeologists would willingly sacrifice their right arm.'

He wondered how he could best express his gratitude.

He had a feeling that unlike most women

she would not be particularly appreciative of jewellery, and it was difficult to think of what else he would offer her.

He had the unmistakable feeling that if he really wished to please her he would leave the cave alone altogether, but that was something he had no intention of doing.

'I will think of a gift she will like when I have the treasure in my hands,' he thought.

If she was astute she would be within her rights in demanding at least half of everything he found.

'If that is what she wants she will be disappointed,' he told himself.

Because he wished, however, to be just, it suddenly struck him that he would have to offer her something from the cave, however hard it might be for him to part with one carving, although it might be small.

With a shrug of his shoulders he told himself that when the time came, doubtless he would know what was the right thing to do without depriving himself and future historians unnecessarily.

Later in the afternoon after he had eaten an excellent luncheon Lord Yelverton fell asleep, and when he awoke he was still worrying about what he should give Tula and had the uncomfortable feeling that in his dreams she had taken from him everything that he prized.

★ ★ ★ ★

The following day Lord Yelverton dressed and walked about on the flat plateau where his tent was pitched.

It seemed to him more beautiful than he had anticipated it would be from what he had seen from his bed.

The stream flowing silver with, in the distance, the cascade enveloped in rainbows was beautiful beyond words, and so were the flowering trees and shrubs growing at the foot of the valley and above them the bare rocks.

There were flowers at the water's edge, and the birds with their brilliant plumage as they came down to drink were part of the colour that seemed in the sunshine almost dazzling.

Lord Yelverton thought that Tula was so much a part of the beauty of the place that it formed a natural background for her, and he found himself looking at her and watching her thinking every moment they were together how different she was from any other woman he had ever known.

He had never particularly admired fair women feeling they were somehow insipid, and most of the women who had aroused his passion over the years had been dark. Elegant, sophisticated, polished until they shone with the glitter and perhaps the hardness of a diamond, they were, he had always told himself, exactly what he admired.

Tula was young, unsophisticated and in some ways very naive, but she was also highly intelligent, knowledgeable on the mythical world of archaeology as well as the positive application of it.

In fact, her knowledge continually surprised Lord Yelverton.

It was she who knew exactly what tools he would require when he went into the cave. It was she who told Jiminez what lantern they should carry with them as well as pick-axes, ropes and spades.

'I suppose,' Lord Yelverton said, 'you knew what your father required when in the past he went digging.'

He remembered that the Curator in Mexico City had said that Audenshaw had been painting for several years, and he thought Tula must have been too young to accompany him when he had last been excavating a site.

Tula had smiled at the question and answered:

'Papa would forget everything that was necessary if I did not look after him. Just as now when he paints outside the Studio he will go off without his brushes or even his canvas unless I give them to him before he leaves the house.'

'He is fortunate to have such a resourceful daughter.'

'Please do not tell him so,' Tula said quickly. 'Like all men, he likes to think he is entirely self-sufficient and has no need for anyone's help or assistance.'

'Are you suggesting that is what I feel?'

'Of course,' Tula said. 'You are resenting everything I want to do for you.'

Because that was true Lord Yelverton had no answer.

Then he laughed.

'You told me not to read your thoughts,' he said, 'and now I suggest you leave mine alone. I find it uncomfortable that you should know what I am thinking.'

There was a long silence before Tula said:

'It is strange how easy it is for me to know what your thoughts are. Sometimes I know what Papa is thinking, but he is far more complicated.'

'Should I take that as a compliment or an insult?' Lord Yelverton asked.

'I do not know,' Tula replied in a puzzled tone. 'When I first saw you and resented that you had come, perhaps to upset Papa, I thought you were a very proud man whom it would be impossible for me to understand.'

She spoke as if she was reasoning it out for herself.

Curious Lord Yelverton enquired:

'What do you feel now?'

'Very...different,' Tula said. 'I understand why you wanted to investigate what is in the cave, and I believe that what you find will be used in the right way and therefore I am no longer...against...you.'

She raised her eyes to Lord Yelverton as she spoke and as they looked at each other, it was difficult to look away.

He had the feeling that although she had not moved she had drawn closer to him and he felt too as if she held him by a spell that was indefinable, and yet very definitely there.

Then downstream some birds took flight as if in sudden fear of an intruder and the quietness that had seemed to envelop them vanished. Lord Yelverton said:

'I now intend to walk up and down at least twenty-five times to strengthen the muscles in my legs.'

'I am sure Diaz would approve,' Tula replied in a quiet tone.

As if she felt he did not want her to watch him, she went into her own tent which was pitched a little way from his.

It was so small that she could not stand upright in it and she lay down on the mattress on which she slept.

Only when she could no longer watch Lord Yelverton walking up and down beside the stream did she lie thinking of him and their marriage which was to take place the following morning.

If Tula lay awake for a long time that night thinking of Lord Yelverton, he also was thinking of her.

He found himself wondering if it was wrong for him to take part in a ceremony which he guessed would mean a great deal to her while in fact it meant nothing to him.

It was all part of the superstitions which he had always deprecated when they encroached on his work, but he had never expected one to envelop him so closely as to involve the ceremony of marriage.

'It is just a matter of words,' he told himself, 'and as reasonable as believing it is unlucky to walk under a ladder, or carrying a piece of white heather for luck!'

'Just mumbo-jumbo!' he added derisively.

Then he checked his thoughts in case Tula should know what he was thinking.

He had told the truth in admitting there was something uncanny about the way he had been pushed into the cascade.

He could only hope fervently that his

marriage would lay the ghost or at least mitigate its power over him, so that he would not be drowned for a second time and Tula with him.

'If she really believes in this marriage,' his conscience told him, 'perhaps the fact that she has taken part in it will prevent her from marrying in the future.'

Lord Yelverton wanted to laugh aloud at the idea. Could anything be more ridiculous or absurd?

Yet he supposed that Diaz, like other uneducated Mexican peasants might believe that such a marriage was binding.

He knew to ask whether this was so would undoubtedly prove embarrassing, and he could only hope that Tula when they went back to her father's house would be too delighted with the treasures they had found to be too concerned with the means which had enabled them to enter the cave.

Lord Yelverton found himself turning the problem over and over in his mind until he fell asleep...

When he awoke to the song of the birds and the first rays of the sun he was so excited at the idea of entering the cave that nothing else seemed of any particular consequence.

Diaz came to shave him and to rub him with the healing oil which Lord Yelverton was now certain had made all the difference to his bruised body.

'You are no longer in pain, *Señor*,' Diaz said, and it was a statement rather than a question.

'No, except when I touch myself the skin is a little tender in certain places,' Lord Yelverton replied. 'Otherwise I am a whole man again, thanks to you and the *Señorita*.'

'That is good!' Diaz said.

Lord Yelverton rose to dress and as he reached for his shirt Diaz put out his hand to stop him.

Lord Yelverton looked at him in surprise and he said:

'Has the *Señorita* Tula not told you what to expect?'

Lord Yelverton shook his head.

'Quetzalcoatl is the god of Rain because rain is what the earth must have to live.'

Lord Yelverton glanced outside at the sunshine and Diaz replied as if he had asked the question:

'As there is no rain you will be married in the spray from the cascade.'

'Very well,' Lord Yelverton agreed. 'What do I wear?'

'I have brought you these, *Señor.*'

Diaz held out the white pantaloons that were worn by all Mexican men.

They looked new and Lord Yelverton was certain they had never been worn before.

He put them on, then wearing nothing else he followed Diaz from the tent out into the sunshine.

Tula was waiting for them and as he saw her he knew she was the very embodiment of the Greek goddess with whom he had identified her from the first moment he had seen her.

She was wearing a white gown of some soft material, but in the Indian fashion it was gathered only by a string over her breasts while her neck and shoulders were bare.

It had a sash around the waist and it reached to the ground where it was embroidered around the hem with the red and green leaves in primitive colours with which the Mexicans decorated their rugs.

She smiled at him, but did not speak.

As they turned to follow behind Diaz who was moving towards the cascade Lord Yelverton was sure that she wore nothing under her gown and he saw that her hair was caught back in the same way as when she had gone riding with him with just a bow of ribbon.

It took them a few minutes to arrive at the cascade with the noise of the water increasing with every step. Then Diaz led the way to a great flat stone that jutted out into the spray.

The water that splashed over it made the moss which covered it wet and it would have been easy for their feet to slip. Lord Yelverton took Tula's hand in his.

Diaz stood on the point of the stone with his back to the cascade while they were facing him, and in a second they were drenched by the spray so that Tula's gown clung to her body.

Diaz began to speak in his quiet, deep voice.

'Barefoot on the living earth with faces to the living rain a man and a woman in the presence of the Morning Star meet to be perfect in one another.'

He looked at Tula.

'Lift your face and say: "This man is my rain from Heaven".'

Tula lifted her face and her eyes were wet with the spray as she repeated:

'This man is my rain from Heaven.'

Diaz looked now at Lord Yelverton.

'Kneel, *Señor,* touch the earth and say: "This woman is the earth to me".'

Lord Yelverton knelt on one knee and laid his hand on the earth as he said:

'This woman is the earth to me.'

He rose and Diaz pointed to Tula, and following his instructions she said slowly and distinctly:

'I, woman, kiss the feet of this man. I will be strength to him and we will be one throughout the long twilight of the Morning Star.'

She knelt, bowed her head and kissed Lord Yelverton's feet, first one and then the other.

On Diaz's instructions Lord Yelverton laid his hand on her hair and said:

'I, man, kiss the brow and touch the head of this woman, and I will be her peace and her increase and we will be one in the long twilight of the Morning Star.'

Then he raised Tula to her feet and kissed her forehead and Diaz put Lord Yelverton's hand over her eyes and her hand over his and said:

'This man has met this woman with his body and the star of his hope, and this woman has met this man with her body and the star of her yearning, and they are one and Quetzalcoatl has blessed them and made them one with the Morning Star.'

Tula and Lord Yelverton took their hands from each other's eyes and as they did so, the light of the sun and the rainbow in the spray seemed to envelop them with an indescribable magic.

For a long moment they looked into each other's eyes and it seemed as if they had journeyed away from the world and were no longer human.

Then Lord Yelverton took Tula's hand to help her back off the stone and onto the path.

Still holding onto each other they walked slowly towards their tents.

Only when they reached them did they divide and still without words went to their own sleeping places.

Tula took off her wet gown and dried her body and her hair and put on her ordinary clothes.

Because she took longer than Lord Yelverton she found when she came from her tent that he, Diaz and Jiminez were already waiting, she thought impatiently, for her.

'I am sorry...' she began.

Without looking at her Lord Yelverton was already beginning the walk once again in the direction of the cascade and the cave at the top of the rocks.

Jiminez and Diaz were carrying the equipment and as they started to climb Tula realized this was because they did not wish Lord Yelverton to exert himself more than was necessary and they also thought that he might have to help her.

She was however quite used to climbing up difficult places and she reached the passage outside the cave at the same moment as Lord Yelverton.

As she pulled herself lithely onto it and

watched him do the same she knew this was the test as to whether the ceremony in which they had just taken part would save him from being assaulted as he had been before.

Apprehensively she watched him pull himself up to his full height, and realized as he did so, that she was between him and the cascade and that Diaz who had just pulled himself up as they had done, was also nearer to the water than they were.

'We are here!' Lord Yelverton remarked as if he reassured himself.

They were the first words any of them had spoken since they had started towards their objective.

He walked to the mouth of the cave and instantly Tula was at his side.

'Let me go first,' she said.

There was a twist to his lips as he replied:

'Sheltering behind a woman's skirts!'

He was half-joking and yet she felt that

there was an element of seriousness in what he had said.

'Very well,' she answered. 'Diaz shall go first. He is dedicated and no follower of Quetzalcoatl would hurt him.'

She raised her voice a little as she spoke the god's name, as if she was warning whoever might be listening.

As she did so Diaz moved in front of them and went into the cave.

Lord Yelverton realized that Tula drew in her breath and he was aware that his heart was beating more excitedly, than when he had discovered the tomb of a Pharaoh in Egypt and a statue in Turkey of the Goddess of Fertility which had lain in the ground for innumerable centuries before he unearthed it.

This was different, and he knew that everything that had taken place already had worked in his emotions and those of the other people with him so that now the moment of achievement was even more thrilling than he had anticipated.

The cave was low but wider than he had expected and at the mouth at any rate, looked not so dirty or filled with fallen rocks as it might have been.

Diaz moved a few feet inside. Then he turned to say:

'I need the lantern.'

Jiminez who had lit it passed it to Lord Yelverton who in turn, passed it to Diaz.

Now they could see by the light of the lantern that the floor of the cave dipped downwards, slanting into the rock and it also rose in height so that even Lord Yelverton could stand upright as long as he was in the centre.

Diaz moved forward and Tula reckoned they must have walked perhaps twenty feet or more before the passage came to an end.

Now what lay in front of them was bricked up and the stones which were not large were obviously laid skilfully against each other to make a barrier.

They all stood for a moment looking

at it. Then Diaz put back his hand and without speaking Jiminez passed forward the pick-axe.

* * * *

Afterwards Tula could never remember how long it had taken to break through the barrier which first Diaz, then Lord Yelverton had done in an expert manner which she knew was the result of long training and experience.

To open a cave hastily might damage irretrievably what it contained and even bring down the roof on their heads if they were not extremely careful.

Both Diaz and Lord Yelverton knew this and as they worked Tula kept out of their way. Jiminez merely leant against the cave walls to watch while handing them in silence everything they required.

The Spaniard had obviously made sure of the safety of his spoils.

The wall had undoubtedly been skilfully

erected for many of the stones were welded together with a substance which had withstood the passage of time and not crumbled to dust as might have been expected.

Stone by stone it was removed and set tidily to one side of the passageway, making a pile first on one side of the opening, then on the other.

As she watched Tula wondered at Lord Yelverton's patience.

She liked the concentrated look on his face and the way he obviously forgot everything but the task he had set himself.

Only when the opening was large enough for them to pass through it without any difficulty did Diaz pick up the lantern that had lain in the passage and lift it high up towards the ceiling.

This was the moment Tula knew when they would find out if all their endeavours had been a waste of time and Lord Yelverton's journey had been unnecessary.

Because it was so tense, so poignant,

she could not help putting out her hand and slipping it into Lord Yelverton's as he stood just behind Diaz waiting to see what the light would reveal.

His hands were dirty from the work he had been doing, and when his fingers closed over her she could feel the excitement vibrating through the whole of his body.

It was what she felt herself, and as her hand rested in his he tightened his grip with the intensity of his feelings until his grasp was painful.

But she would have endured far greater pain in knowing that in this if in no other way, they were one as Diaz had made them in their marriage in the spray.

★ ★ ★ ★

It would have been dark in the tent except for the stars coming out in the sky above and the moonlight, which while touching the cascade had not yet reached the valley.

Lord Yelverton was lying on his bed and Tula had brought him a drink before she retired to her own tent.

'You are tired?' she said.

'I will not tell a lie,' he smiled. 'I am tired, but far too excited to sleep.'

Tula laughed.

'Will any of us be able to do that tonight?'

'I do not remember ever before being so thrilled,' Lord Yelverton said. 'For one moment I thought there was nothing there. Then I understood.'

'We might have guessed that the Spaniard would have stolen only small pieces, unless he was to draw attention to himself.'

'It never struck me that would be likely until we were inside the cave,' Lord Yelverton replied. 'But I should have known from the jaguar bone and the amber, that the things he took under the noses of his compatriots would be small but valuable.'

There was silence for a moment as both

Lord Yelverton and Tula were thinking of the bones they had found, the jade, alabaster, pearl, coral and rock crystal, all exquisitely carved as his first piece of amber had been.

Packed in small bags which had crumbled away through the years, they had at first seemed to be insignificant, when they had expected something large, bulky and impressive.

It was only when they had brushed aside the dust that they realized the value of their findings was inestimable, and that the brilliance of the Mixtec craftsmen whose work was known to be finer than that of any others was represented here in a collection that was unique in the whole history of archaeology.

As Diaz was to say later, every piece had a religious significance and apart from anything else was hitherto unknown to those who had been studying a civilization that had been lost at Monte Albán.

Diaz himself was more thrilled with the

different representations of Quetzalcoatl which he was sure had been used in the Pyramid of the sun.

It might take those who studied the hieroglyphics some time to decipher and interpret all that was found, but in the meantime each piece was so beautiful that Tula could only touch them with reverent fingers, and know that they had been part of the dedication and worship of the god.

After they had spent a long time in the cave, Lord Yelverton placed very carefully the majority of the small pieces in a bag which Jiminez had brought with him.

'These should be enough for us to examine and talk about for today,' he said. 'Tomorrow we will come back for more. I suppose it is safe to leave the cave unattended?'

Diaz smiled.

'You have already had experience, *Señor*, of how well it is guarded.'

Lord Yelverton had actually forgotten that while they had been allowed to enter unmolested another intruder might be treated in the same way that he had been.

'You are right, Diaz,' he said. 'We need not worry ourselves on that score.'

Carrying the bag himself, because he would trust no-one else with it, Lord Yelverton climbed slowly and carefully down the rocks.

They had been longer there than they had planned and by the time Jiminez had cooked them a meal the afternoon was almost spent and the sun was losing its heat.

Afterwards as Jiminez tidied up Lord Yelverton brought the treasures from his bag and having wiped them carefully with a silk handkerchief, laid them on the grass in front of Tula and Diaz.

In the daylight they were even more beautiful than they had seemed in the cave.

Everything about them was perfect from the purity of the crystal to the pink of the coral and the translucence of the alabaster.

Some pieces were ornamented with pearls, but Lord Yelverton knew that what would really be more interesting to historians than anything else, was what was carved on the jaguar bones, and Diaz agreed with him.

He looked at them for a long time and Lord Yelverton said:

'Tomorrow, Diaz, after we bring out what is left in the cave, I want you to choose a piece for yourself, or rather for your work, as I know that will matter to you more than anything else.'

Because he spoke in such an understanding manner Tula looked at him with what he knew was an expression of gratitude.

'You mean that, *Señor?*' Diaz asked in a low voice.

'Of course I mean it,' Lord Yelverton replied, 'and the choice is entirely yours. It is not a question of value, but I think you will know which one appeals to you most, because of its sanctity and what part it had played in the past.'

For a moment Diaz did not speak. Then his eyes met Lord Yelverton's and he said:

'You have been blessed, my son. You have seen the Morning Star and it will never leave you.'

The words were strangely moving. Then, as if his feelings overcame him he rose and moved away in silence, and they knew as they saw him go towards the cascade that he evoked Quetzalcoatl in the spray that represented him as god of rain.

Without saying any more Lord Yelverton put the treasures back in the bag and only when he had taken them into his tent did Tula say:

'It would be wise to go to bed. It has been a long day full of emotion, and you must not suffer a relapse after Diaz and I have worked so hard to make you well again.'

'I think you are talking sense,' Lord Yelverton conceded.

As she moved away from the opening of his tent he undressed and lay down thankfully on the mattress.

★ ★ ★ ★

Jiminez brought him his dinner later and after the sun had gone down he wondered why he had been left alone until Tula came into his tent.

'What have you been doing?' he asked.

'Thinking,' she replied, 'and I suppose, reliving the excitement we have all experienced.'

'And have you forgiven me for disturbing what you thought should have been left alone for at least another thousand years?' Lord Yelverton asked.

'I was wrong,' Tula said simply. 'Diaz knew, as I did not, that what you would find would benefit the world, or at least those who want to understand what

Quetzalcoatl and the other gods can teach them.'

Lord Yelverton smiled.

'I admit that when I came here that was not my idea of what I had to do. I was, I thought, merely an archaeologist rattling dry bones for the sake of history.'

'And now?' Tula asked.

'Now, like you, I am thinking that perhaps what I have found will add not only to the knowledge of mankind, but perhaps to their minds, their hearts and their souls.'

Tula drew a deep breath.

'That is what I wanted you to think.'

'And perhaps you have willed me into believing it.'

'No, no,' she said quickly. 'You have found it for yourself, it was nothing to do with me!'

'It has a great deal to do with you, Tula!'

It was growing dark in the tent and her head was silhouetted against the starlight outside and he thought it made her look like a piece of the rock crystal.

'I want to know something,' Lord Yelverton said.

'What is it?' Tula enquired.

'What did you feel when we were being married in that strange way? What I felt was certainly not what I had expected.'

She did not answer, and Lord Yelverton reached out to take her hand in his.

He felt her quiver as he touched her and said insistently:

'Tell me what you felt.'

'As if it was very real...and very true that the...spirit of creation passed from the water of the cascade into...us and we were a part of it.'

'I thought the same,' Lord Yelverton answered, 'and it was not what I expected to feel. At that moment you and I were very close.'

As he finished speaking he raised her hand to his lips.

For a moment his mouth lingered on

the softness of her skin.

Then she made a little sound he could not describe or interpret.

Her hand slipped from his and swiftly as a bird flying over the stream outside, she was gone.

Alone, Lord Yelverton lay for a long time looking at the moonlight.

6

Tula sat on the grass staring at the precious objects which Lord Yelverton had placed on the ground in front of him.

There were thirty in all and they realized there must have been thirty-four originally, counting the four which the seaman had stolen.

All these had been on a kind of shelf which was just inside the cave and it was easy to understand how the seaman had made a hole just large enough for his hand and by reaching through, had managed to take the first four objects nearest to the blocked opening.

They had also found there was a great heap of what appeared to be dust on the floor of the cave.

They eventually realized this must have

been the remains of the clothes the Spaniard had left behind him which had during the centuries crumbled away until nothing remained but his gold buttons and the bridle of his horse which he must have used for ceremonial occasions, with gold embossed stirrups to match.

These, Lord Yelverton knew, would be prized by the Museum in Mexico City where he had decided to send them after they had been on exhibition in Europe.

But he gave Jiminez two of the Spaniard's gold buttons which delighted him so much that he was speechless and unable to express his thanks.

Diaz had taken a long time choosing what he should have, trying first to decipher the inscriptions on many of the treasures of alabaster and coral, besides jade which must have originally been brought into the country by sailors from the Orient.

No jade artefacts had been found in Mexico and there were no deposits of that stone in the country, but the jade was very valuable and very beautiful.

It was fascinating to speculate how it could have reached the Mixtecs who had utilized it as they had every other sort of substance in the worship of their gods.

It had become very hot in the middle of the day, but now it was growing cooler and the sun was losing its strength.

When Jiminez, clasping his gold buttons in his hand, had left them, Lord Yelverton said to Diaz:

'Now it is your turn.'

One by one Diaz lifted the precious objects and Lord Yelverton was aware that he was not only looking at them but feeling the vibrations that came from them.

He was silent and Lord Yelverton saw that Tula's eyes were fixed on Diaz as if she too, was trying to understand which, from the point of view of their faith, was the most important of the objects they had discovered.

They had all got very dirty while they were searching through the huge pile of dust for small pieces of gold braid or other remnants of the decoration which must once have been on the ornate garments to be used on festive or ceremonial occasions.

Lord Yelverton thought that in going back for more treasures the Spaniard would have taken as little as possible with him, and in what safer place could he deposit his clothes, as well as his other treasures, than in a cave that was guarded by the spirit of the man he had killed?

Diaz finally made up his mind.

'If the *Señor* will permit me,' he said in his quiet, deep voice, 'and if you do not want it for yourself, I would like to have the jaguar bone which first brought you here.'

Lord Yelverton smiled.

'I feel it has a special significance for you, as it has for me,' he said. 'It has a way of drawing one's attention, whether one wishes it or not.'

'That is what I feel,' Diaz said simply,

'and thank you, *Señor,* the gods will bless you for your generosity.'

He rose to his feet and said:

'Do not be disturbed if you hear my voice during the night. I intend that this sacred bone shall release the spirit that has been earth-bound.'

He walked away and Lord Yelverton looked to Tula for explanation.

'I believe there are ceremonies that can free a spirit from his vow,' she said. 'The Catholic Church calls it "Exorcism", but here it is very different.'

'That is something else I have to learn,' Lord Yelverton answered. 'There is so much that I feel I could stay here for a thousand years and still find there is more.'

Tula gave a little laugh.

'The Mexicans have an expression which describes exactly what you are trying to say. It is: *"Como Mexico no hay dos."*'

' "There is only one Mexico!" ' Lord Yelverton translated.

'Exactly!' Tula said.

He looked down at the treasures that lay between them.

'I think we should pack these up,' he said, 'and tomorrow we will take them and show them to your father. I am sure he will find them very exciting.'

Tula gave a little sigh.

'I think too he will regret that he was not with us. I shall never forget that moment when you walked into the cave half-expecting to be thrown out of it, and saw these wonderful treasures lying on the shelf.'

'I thought I must be dreaming,' Lord Yelverton said. 'I was afraid that after all our expectations we should be disappointed.'

'So was I,' Tula smiled, 'and it would have been too bitter to bear after you were nearly...drowned.'

There was a little throb in her voice which he found very moving.

'Thanks to you I am alive and of course,

Tula, any of these that you wish to own are yours.'

Her eyes widened and he knew incredibly that she had not expected him to give her anything.

'But of course,' he said, 'I intend to present you with a gift that will commemorate what has been an unforgettable experience for us both.'

'I need...nothing,' Tula said quickly. 'As you say, it has been an unforgettable experience and I shall never...forget it.'

He knew because he could read her thoughts that she was thinking not of the caves, but of the moment they had been married in the spray from the cascade.

Because he did not wish to dwell on that he said lightly:

'I had thought of giving you diamonds, but now I feel that coral is what you should possess, or perhaps this.'

He picked up as he spoke a piece of jade that had been exquisitely carved and ornamented with pearls.

Because they had been buried for so long some of them had lost their sheen and looked a little sickly, but Lord Yelverton was certain that if they were handled, or better still worn next to the skin, they would revive.

He wondered if he should suggest to Tula that she should take the jade to bed with her. Then he thought it might seem too intimate a suggestion.

Her eyes met his and he knew that she was aware of what he was thinking.

'I think they will come back to life in the sun,' she said.

'I hope so,' he answered. 'If not, you must give them life, as you gave it to me.'

There was silence while Tula no longer looked at him but at the jade he held in his hand.

'I think we should wait and find out if your father can read anything that is written on these things,' Lord Yelverton said. 'Perhaps we may find one that will be particularly applicable to you.'

He smiled before he added:

'The first time we talked together you might have been affiliated to the Moon Goddess.'

As if she was shy Tula rose to her feet.

'Although I have washed my hands and face,' she said, 'I still feel dirty after all that dust, and I am going to bathe in the spray from the cascade.'

She walked away before Lord Yelverton could reply that he would like to go with her. Then he told himself it might make her shy.

Later, before they had finished their evening meal, the sun had set and darkness came quickly.

One moment the sky was translucent and vivid with colour, then the first evening star quivered above the cascade and soon the night was brilliant with them.

With a glass of wine in his hand, Lord Yelverton leant back against the trunk of a tree under which they had eaten their meal and sighed with contentment.

'How could I have guessed when I left Mexico City in search of your father, that I should find not only the treasures I sought, but a door opening onto a new world I had no idea existed.'

Tula looked at him for an explanation, and he went on:

'Your world, in which I am now prepared to believe: a world that as you told me, is peculiarly Mexico with its magic and witchcraft, its devils and sorcerers.'

'You have forgotten its gods and angels,' Tula said quickly.

'Of course,' he said, 'and that is what you have been—my good angel who not only saved my life, but with your magic-wand gave me the desire of my heart.'

'And now you will live happily ever afterwards.'

'I think that having climbed the highest mountain, reached the top and brought off the greatest prize, I should stop,' Lord

Yelverton said. 'Anything else would be an anti-climax. But then what else can I do?'

He knew the answer without waiting for Tula to reply.

There was plenty of work waiting for him in England with his house, his estate, the family of which he was the head. Yet it all seemed rather pale beside the excitement of discovery and making the long-dead past live again.

Because he was deep in his thoughts there was silence for a little while. Then mingling with the soft roar of the cascade there came the sound of a human voice.

They both knew that it was Diaz chanting in the cave and Jiminez would be with him.

His tone was rhythmic and monotonous, and it seemed to Lord Yelverton to blend with his own feelings and the mystery of the night.

Music has always been an expression of deep emotion which cannot be said in words, and Lord Yelverton wondered what music he would use if at this moment he could express what he was feeling, and his gratitude to Tula.

'Diaz will chant all night,' she said, 'and every note and every word will gradually release the bonds which hold the sacrificed man prisoner. At dawn he will be free to join his loved ones.'

The way she spoke was so simple and yet so profound in its belief, that Lord Yelverton felt himself moved by it.

'Do you really believe that?' he enquired.

'Yes.'

'Then no-one will suffer as I did being hurled from the cave into the cascade.'

'There will be no need now the cave is empty.'

It all sounded like practical common sense if he could accept the explanation of how the cave was being supernaturally guarded in the first place.

In the starlight with the music of the water and the chanting in the distance, he thought it would be difficult to disbelieve anything that Tula told him.

As if she was thinking of him, she said:

'You are tired and you must go to bed.'

Lord Yelverton put down his empty glass.

'I suppose you are right,' he said. 'And I am eager for tomorrow to come so that I can see your father's face when he learns what we have brought back with us.'

'If you are thinking only of him,' Tula replied, 'you will tell him you have found nothing.'

'How can I do such a thing?' Lord Yelverton expostulated. 'Your father is without exception the greatest authority in the whole world on the ancient civilization of Mexico. I know that you think he is happy painting, but I think it is the most regrettable and almost unforgivable waste of his great talent.'

'You do not understand.'

'What is there to understand?' Lord Yelverton asked sharply.

'When my mother died,' Tula replied, 'Papa was like a madman. I was very young at the time, but I have learnt that those who were with him thought he might kill himself!'

Lord Yelverton looked at her in astonishment.

'Is that true?'

'Yes,' Tula answered, 'and it was perhaps only because he loved me that he could not kill himself, as my nurse found him trying to do one evening.'

'I cannot believe it!' Lord Yelverton said beneath his breath.

He had thought Audenshaw was a strange, eccentric character, but that he should be so uncontrolled and unrestrained was almost an insult to his nationality.

'At first he drank,' Tula said in an impersonal voice, as if she was telling the history of someone with whom she was not personally concerned.

Lord Yelverton with a new perception realized that because she was involved so deeply she could not speak of her father's suffering unless she made it seem an ordinary tale.

He was also certain that this was the first time she had spoken of it to any outsider, and because he was deeply interested he did not wish to interrupt.

'When he found that made him ill,' Tula went on, 'he chose a different way to try and forget.'

Lord Yelverton knew without her putting it into words that this had been women.

He could see the long succession of women who had lived with Audenshaw, who were doubtless genuinely in love with him, while to him they were only a narcotic, a drug to make him forget what he had lost.

'Later,' Tula continued, 'we wandered from place to place, and Papa was so restless that no-one knew from one day to another whether he would stay, or go.'

There was no need for her to put into words how hard it had been. Then to Lord Yelverton's surprise she said:

'Then because he thought it would please Mama he sent me away.'

'Where did you go?'

'To Florence.'

This was so surprising that for the moment Lord Yelverton could hardly believe that she was telling him the truth.

He had never for a moment suspected that Tula had ever been to Europe or known any other life outside Acapulco, or certainly not beyond the parts explored by her father where he had written his book on the Aztecs.

'I was there for a year and a half,' Tula was saying. 'I only came back because Papa was in such a muddle with the children, and finding it difficult to get anyone to look after them.'

'But you were too young for such responsibility,' Lord Yelverton said sharply.

'I managed,' Tula answered. 'Then

when I met Miss Webber—Liza we call her—everything was much easier. It was she who found teachers for Lucette and schools for the others, and now Papa has settled down it makes everything far more simple.'

At last Lord Yelverton could understand why Tula was afraid he might make her father restless again.

'What do you want me to do?' he asked.

'I suppose we will have to show Papa what you have found,' Tula conceded. 'It would be cruel not to do so. But you must convince him there are not likely to be other caves with similar carvings waiting for him...or for you.'

'From my point of view that is easy,' Lord Yelverton said. 'I was planning to go back to England.'

'Of course.'

Tula rose from where she had been sitting and walked slowly across the soft ground to the edge of the stream.

The stars were bright overhead, but she stood looking down as if she thought she could still see the small fish darting over the rocky surface as she had in the sunshine.

Lord Yelverton joined her.

He stood for a moment looking not at the water, but at her.

He was thinking that she was as lovely as she had seemed that first night when he had seen her looking up at the stars and she had been thinking of Quetzalcoatl and trying to understand the mysteries of the Heavens.

'I have another suggestion,' he said at last.

'What is it?' she enquired in a low voice, but she did not turn towards him.

'Why do we not, because we are so lucky together, try to find another treasure trove in Yukatan?'

His lips were smiling as he went on:

'Your people, the Tolmecs, invaded Yukatan after they had been driven out of the valley of Mexico, and they took there the worship of Quetzalcoatl.'

'I knew this,' Tula said, 'but I am surprised that you should.'

'I learned a little before I came here,' Lord Yelverton replied, 'and I have learned a great deal more from you.'

Tula did not speak, and he went on:

'We work well together and since you have brought me back to life I think I have been happier than at any other time in my life, despite my injuries.'

He moved nearer to Tula as he said:

'Surely it is a waste and perhaps a crime for us to leave each other now, for me to go back to England, while you stay here, when we might be together?'

His voice seemed to linger on the last word and it had a caressing note which had not been there in anything he had said before.

Tula raised her head to look at him.

'What are you...saying?' she asked in a voice little above a whisper.

'I am saying this,' Lord Yelverton answered.

He put his arms around her as he spoke and drew her close against him.

Then his mouth was on hers.

He knew as he did so that her lips were exactly as he expected them to be, cool and soft, inexperienced and innocent.

At the same time the touch of them gave him a strange rapture he had never known before in the whole of his life.

He had kissed many women, but perhaps never one for the first time, and now holding Tula in his arms, he felt an inexpressible excitement.

Yet there was also a gentleness that was unlike his usual feeling for any woman he desired.

To Tula he gave her the same feeling of sanctity which she had known when they were being married in the spray and which to her had been a moment of complete spiritual dedication.

Lord Yelverton's arms tightened.

'You are so beautiful, quite unlike anyone I have ever seen before,' he said, 'and I want you—I want you desperately! You know as well as I do, that I cannot live without you.'

He did not wait for her reply but was kissing her again; kissing her with passionate, demanding, possessive kisses which made her his, so that she became a part of him.

Only when he raised his head to look down into her face, very lovely in the moonlight, with her eyes dark and mysterious, did he say:

'You will come with me!'

It was a statement more than a question, and he was sure there was no possibility of her refusing...

He felt her quiver against him.

'I love you!' he said, and knew as he spoke that it was true. He loved her as he had never expected to love any woman.

Then Tula's hands were on his chest pushing him a little way from her.

'You are tired. You must go to bed.'

'I want to make sure of you first.'

'We will talk about it tomorrow.'

'Why not now?'

'I have to...think.'

'There is no reason why you should think. I will do the thinking. We will go to Yukatan together. Your father will not mind because, as you have told me already, there is someone to look after him and the children, and we shall be so happy that it will be a long time before there is any reason for me to return to England.'

Tula was free of him.

'Sleep well,' she said softly. 'The music of the cascade will send you to sleep.'

'Only your lips can do that,' Lord Yelverton wanted to reply.

But already Tula had left him, moving silently and swiftly, like a white ghost under the trees towards her tent.

For a moment he was annoyed that she had left him.

He wanted to kiss her again. He wanted

to make certain she understood what he required of her.

Then he realized that he was in fact, very tired. As Tula had said, it had been an exciting day and an emotional one, especially the last few minutes of it.

He could still feel her in his arms, and the softness of her body against his.

'She is lovely, absolutely lovely!' he thought. 'We will be very happy together in Yukatan.'

As he undressed he thought that Yukatan was to all intents and purposes, an undeveloped world from an archaeological point of view, and he had always heard there were ruins as yet unexplored as fine, if not finer, than those near Mexico City.

He had also been told that the messages carved into the huge rocks which had been excavated, were of a language no-one could read.

'If anyone can help me in this new quest,' Lord Yelverton thought, 'it will be Tula.'

He lay down on his mattress and put his treasures beside him, feeling almost as if they were speaking to him, telling him something he ought to understand, but which was beyond his comprehension.

'There is so much research to be done on these alone,' he thought.

It struck him that he should really take them back to England first before he embarked on another expedition.

But because he knew that for the moment he so much wanted to be with Tula that he could not leave her, it seemed an excellent idea to take her to Yukatan.

'We shall be very happy,' he told himself with a smile before he fell asleep.

* * * *

Tula had not undressed and she was not lying down. Instead she was sitting in the opening of her tent, looking up at the stars.

She had never known such ecstasy or

such rapture as the moment when Lord Yelverton had kissed her and her love which had been there in her heart, burst like an hibiscus bud into the fullness of its beauty.

'I love him! I love him!' she whispered, feeling that her voice was caught up into the skies.

At the same time she knew what he had offered her was only what her father offered the many women who had come and gone since her mother died.

She had not contemplated that Lord Yelverton would propose marriage, yet behind the intensity of her need for him there was the unspoken fear that this was just a transitory emotion.

When his desire had burnt itself out, it would mean that she would return home, while he left for England.

She was not shocked, she was not even surprised. It was, she thought, inevitable when he had seen the way her father lived and her acceptance of his behaviour.

She knew then that while it would crucify her to lose Lord Yelverton she could not do what he wanted. Whether he knew it or not, she belonged to him for the rest of her life.

Their marriage in the spray had been as real for her as any vow she could have taken before the high altar in Mexico Cathedral.

They had been joined as man and wife by Quetzalcoatl and the blessing of the Morning Star had been given them, and nothing said or done by man could undo it.

'I will be a strength to him,' Tula whispered, her face turned towards the Heavens, 'throughout the long twilight of the Morning Star.'

That meant as far as she was concerned until her time on earth was finished.

Because what she had said was to her a sacred vow she would never allow any other man to touch her and no man but Lord Yelverton could be her husband.

'He does not understand,' she mur-mured.

She did not speak with any bitterness, nor did she blame him.

She only knew that just as Diaz, chanting in the cave, believed that his prayers would release the soul of the man who had been imprisoned there for three hundred years, so while she lived she belonged to Lord Yelverton.

He might not be aware of it; he might love and marry in his own faith, a dozen women; but as far as she was concerned, she was his wife, and for her there was no escape from her vow.

Finally, as she lay down inside the tent and shut her eyes, Tula felt as if she was close against Lord Yelverton's heart.

She could feel the ecstasy his lips had given her, ripple through her like the life-force she had poured from her own body into his.

'I have given him the breath of life,' she thought, 'and because of it he is mine. Our lives have merged, and we are one.'

For the moment she was radiantly content with the spiritual wonder of it.

Yet some sensible, logical part of her mind knew the agony that would come when Lord Yelverton left her, and she was alone without him.

★ ★ ★ ★

When she awoke early in the morning Tula wondered how she could bear to let Lord Yelverton go without belonging to him not only with her heart and with her soul, but also with her body.

'It is his,' she murmured.

At the same time she knew with a different part of herself that she could not sink to the level of the women who came to her father without a thought of anything but their physical satisfaction.

She knew they were not interested in his brain, his vast knowledge, or anything except the fact that he was an extraordinarily attractive man, and their desire for him burnt like a fire.

'Lord Yelverton must go back to England,' Tula decided.

While her whole being cried out at the pain of parting from him, she knew it was the right thing for him to do.

She was dressed soon after dawn and began to cook the breakfast. When Lord Yelverton joined her she said:

'I suggest we leave as soon as possible, and when we get home you can instruct your own servants to call here and pack up the tents.'

'A good idea!' Lord Yelverton replied.

'I think Diaz and Jiminez will still be asleep, so it would be kinder to leave without trying to say goodbye. They only finished chanting when the morning broke and they must be very tired.'

'Let us hope they have achieved what they set out to do,' Lord Yelverton answered.

He was not particularly interested, and

as soon as they had finished breakfast, they saddled the horses and set off down the hill towards Acapulco.

Because there was no need to pass through the village to call on the *Curandera*, they took a much quicker route than they had used before.

It was steep and the loose stones on the rocks were sharp and dangerous, but the horses were sure-footed, even though they were fresh.

When they reached the house they saw Ajax Audenshaw coming through the shrubs from the direction of the sea.

He had obviously been swimming and he waved a greeting to Tula who went to him and put her arms around his neck.

'Are you all right, Papa? There have been no difficulties while I have been away?'

'None at all! Liza has looked after us admirably, but I am glad to have you back.'

She kissed him, then without saying any

more, walked into the house.

It was left to Lord Yelverton to explain what had happened and to show Audenshaw the treasures.

When he inspected them the older man forgot his painting and became wholly an archaeologist.

He turned piece after piece over in his hands, translated some of the writing on them but confessed that he was puzzled by most of the rest.

'I congratulate you, Yelverton!' he said at last. 'I can hardly bear to think that this was sitting right on my doorstep, so to speak, and I had no idea of it!'

'I could not have found it without Tula.'

'I thought she would help.'

'She also saved my life!'

Lord Yelverton did not explain exactly why he had fallen into the cascade because he wanted to minimize the effect it had had on him, but Audenshaw had already learned from the servants who brought up their tents that he had been injured.

'Diaz was with you,' he said. 'I have already heard of his powers of healing. He is a strange man. I presume you know he is a follower of Quetzalcoatl?'

'Yes, he told me,' Lord Yelverton answered.

'It is extraordinary how many people there are in different parts of Mexico who worship that particular god,' Audenshaw remarked. 'What you have found will add greatly to their knowledge of him. He was one of the most pleasant of all their different deities.'

Then Audenshaw tried to decipher many of the signs and to deduce from the shape of the different pieces of precious stone what part they had played in the ceremonies in which they had been used.

When luncheon was ready, to Lord Yelverton's surprise, there was no sign of Tula.

'Go and fetch the *Señorita* Tula,' Audenshaw ordered one of the servants.

'The *Señorita* ask if the *Señor* will excuse her,' the man replied. 'She is washing her hair and too busy to come to luncheon.'

Audenshaw laughed.

'There speaks the eternal woman!' he said. 'You achieve a world-shattering discovery and she is thinking of her appearance!'

'She is entitled to do that,' Lord Yelverton answered. 'She nursed me very ably while I was too bruised to move about.'

'Tula is very good at nursing,' Ajax Audenshaw answered, 'but I have been thinking while you were away that she ought to live a very different sort of life. So I have been making plans.'

'What sort of plans?'

There was a frown between Lord Yelverton's eyes which Audenshaw did not notice as he answered:

'I think she should visit her mother's family in Ireland. They suggested it two years ago after I brought her back from

238

Florence, but I refused because selfishly I wanted her to set my own house in order.'

'Which I understand she did most efficiently.'

'Of course,' Audenshaw agreed. 'But when she stayed with you by the cascade, I knew it was something her mother would not have allowed, nor her grandfather, the Earl of Kilkerry.'

Lord Yelverton stiffened.

As if he had asked the question Ajax Audenshaw said:

'Did you not know that my wife was one of the Irish O'Kerrys? I thought you might have sensed the Celt in Tula.'

'I realized she was unusually perceptive,' Lord Yelverton said in a low voice.

'Are the Irish ever anything else?' Audenshaw enquired. 'I fell in love with Tula's mother the moment I saw her. She said it was fate that brought us together, or perhaps it was the leprechauns!'

He laughed.

'Whatever the explanation, we were married three weeks after we first met to the fury of the Earl, who had very different ideas for his beautiful daughter.'

There was a note in Audenshaw's voice that Lord Yelverton knew meant there was longing for his dead wife in a manner that was so emotionally revealing that he felt as if he was intruding on something very private.

Then Audenshaw said abruptly:

'Tula will go to Ireland, and I shall have no argument about it. In fact now I think of it, perhaps you would be kind enough to look after her on the journey. It is a long way for a young girl to travel alone.'

He took Lord Yelverton's acceptance as a matter of course and did not wait for his answer.

Instead he picked up a piece of the jade and started to speak of the masks discovered in some of the pyramids which had intrigued those who tried to explain how jade had come into Mexico in the first place.

* * * *

Tula, having washed her hair, was drying it in the sunshine.

There was a balcony attached to her bedroom, only a small one but of beautifully wrought iron, a style which the Spaniards had incorporated in the houses they built in Mexico.

She sat with her back to the view of the sea and the sunshine on her head was so warm that it seemed to burn right through her body.

She was not actually thinking of herself, but of Lord Yelverton, wondering what he would think when she told him she would not do what he asked, and wondering how she could refuse without hurting him or letting him know that she loved him.

That she would have to say goodbye when he left, knowing she would never

241

see him again, would be like cutting off an arm or a leg, and once he had gone she knew she would never be a whole person again.

But she could not spoil the beauty and the sacredness of what to her was a perfect moment of time which was engraved forever on her heart.

She had known before Diaz had suggested it that if they were married the Guardian of the cave would be unable to hurt him. When she had stood beside him in the spray and Diaz had married them in the beautiful words of the Marriage Service of Quetzalcoatl, she felt as if the god himself was near them.

In the touch of the spray he blessed them in their living and breathing for all time.

To the followers of Quetzalcoatl the Morning Star was perhaps the most sacred emblem. It was a part of every ceremony and almost every prayer.

One stanza had been translated from the walls of what was left of his pyramid and both her father and Diaz had recited it to Tula:

'But the sons of God come and go
They come from beyond the Morning Star;
And thither they return from the land
of men.'

Tula had often repeated it to herself. Then a year later Diaz had brought her three more lines.

How he knew such things she never could quite understand, but she felt there was a way of communication among the Priests of Quetzalcoatl which was not revealed to the ordinary people.

It was only because Diaz loved her and knew how sincere she was in her feelings towards the god he worshipped that he talked to her as he would never have spoken to any other foreigner.

They had met on the side of the mountain when Tula was out riding and as if he could not help sharing with her the elation which came from the information that had been carried to him, almost as soon as they sat down to talk, he told her what he had learned.

'This comes from the ritual worship of the god,' he said proudly.

> *'Those who follow me must cross the mountains of the sky,*
> *And pass the houses of the stars by night.*
> *They shall find me only in the Morning Star.'*

When she had been married Tula had felt that for a moment she was swept into the sky, that Lord Yelverton went with her, and they found the Morning Star and they were in it as it was within them.

Now she knew that to Lord Yelverton it had not meant the same and, as she had half-suspected from the beginning, although he denied it he had only been play-acting, so that he could reach the cave and obtain his heart's desire.

He had been safe because through her their marriage had been accepted.

But now he did not feel married, nor that the blessing of Quetzalcoatl was binding upon him.

'I am his wife,' Tula said to herself wistfully, 'but he is not my husband.'

She felt the tears come into her eyes, but she would not shed them.

She told herself that she had been fortunate to find him, living isolated, as it were, in Acapulco.

Only fate, and perhaps Quetzalcoatl himself, had brought her the one man who could ever matter to her into her world, almost as if he had dropped from the Morning Star itself.

He had come, she had known him, she had saved his life, and he had kissed her.

That should be enough, Tula thought, and she would be greedy to ask for more.

And yet it was impossible to deny that her whole body reached out towards him with a cry so primitive, so fundamental, that it might have come from the earth itself.

It was Eve calling to Adam, seeking the man belonging to her since the beginning of eternity, and to whom she would belong until the seas ran dry.

'After tomorrow I shall never see him again,' Tula thought.

And now she could no longer prevent the tears, hot and exquisitely painful, from running down her cheeks.

7

Later in the day Tula found there were a great many things for her to do that had been forgotten while she was away.

She was busy with Liza sorting out the children's clothes and when they returned from school she found she had a number of their problems to solve which, if not of very great importance, seemed to take up a lot of time.

She was aware that Lord Yelverton was with her father and when Carlotta arrived to model for him, he sent her away and was obviously not interested in anything except the antiquities.

It worried Tula in case it was making him feel that he must go back to his own excavations, and if he did, she wondered if she would have to stay alone with the children in Acapulco, or whether he would want them to accompany them.

'There are too many of us,' she thought almost despairingly, 'and besides what would happen to their education?'

She looked so worried that Liza smiled at her.

'Leave me to do the worrying, Tula,' she said. 'Things solve themselves and the children have been very good while you have been away.'

'I know that,' Tula said, 'and I am very grateful to you.'

'There is no need to be,' Liza replied, 'I love coming here and to tell the truth, I am lonely in my little house down in the village.'

She looked out of the window at the palm trees and the flowers and said softly:

'This is like home. Everywhere I looked in Devon it was beautiful like this.'

Tula wanted to say impulsively that as far as she was concerned she could stay for ever.

Then she thought she must ask her father first.

Perhaps he would think that another woman in the house was a bore, but Liza was so understanding.

She was obviously not shocked by Dolores and the children loved her, from Petronella who always wanted to be rocked in her arms, to Lucette who listened when she made her tidy her hair and take off the more flamboyant of her clothes.

'We all love you, Liza,' Tula said simply, and saw the older woman's face flush with pleasure.

When she learnt later in the afternoon that Lord Yelverton and her father had left the house, Tula felt a little piqued that they had not asked her to go with them.

She did not know where they had gone, whether it was to the cave or to Acapulco.

She only felt as if she had been deserted, and as there seemed to be nothing more to do, she walked into the garden to stand at the cliff's edge as she had done the first night when Lord Yelverton had come to her, when she was looking at the stars.

She had thought she was angry with him then, but she knew now it was not anger but fear—fear because he was so handsome, and she supposed instinctively she had been afraid of falling in love with him.

Now that had happened.

She loved him until he filled the whole Universe and wherever she looked there was nothing but him.

After a long time she walked back to the house and found once again that her father and Lord Yelverton were together in the Studio.

'They do not want me,' she thought wistfully. 'At the same time, if it had not been for me they would not now have the pleasure of inspecting the beautiful carvings we found in the cave or be trying to decipher what is written on them.'

She wondered if she should take Lord

Yelverton at his word and choose one for herself.

Then she thought she needed no memento or souvenir of his visit to remind her of him.

She would always remember that moment in the spray when they had been married, and when he had kissed her. She knew that twice they travelled together towards the stars, and she was his for all eternity.

'I love him! I love him!' she thought again.

Because the tears came into her eyes she hastily went up to her bedroom in case she should meet anyone and they would see she was crying for the moon.

Now he would leave, she thought, and imagined that already his servants, having collected his tents from the cascade would be packing them away onto the mules and horses with which he had arrived in Acapulco.

'I must say goodbye with dignity,' she

251

thought. 'He must never know how much I mind him leaving, or how much I love him. He would never admire a woman who was uncontrolled or over-emotional, like Dolores.'

Then she knew that if she were like Dolores she would go with Lord Yelverton as he had asked her to do.

She could imagine nothing more like Heaven than to be in Yukatan with him.

They would work all day clearing the pyramids and tombs which she had been told were thickly covered by the jungle, but the outline of them could be seen amongst the tropical vegetation.

And at night they would be together under the stars.

Tula drew in her breath at the thought.

She knew now how strong his arms were and that his lips could ignite not only a rapture and a wonder beyond expression, but also a fire that she would feel flickering through her body until it reached her lips.

She was so intent on her thought of Lord Yelverton that she was startled when there was a knock on the door.

'What is it?' she asked.

'The *Señor* asks me to tell you that dinner will be a little early tonight,' one of the servants replied.

'Thank you,' Tula said. 'I will not be late.'

She thought she could guess why her father had ordered dinner early, and it was like a stab in her breast.

It meant that Lord Yelverton was leaving at dawn tomorrow morning.

It was usual for travellers to do so, so that they could make a good start in the cool of the day, and then when it grew really hot, both they and their horses could rest under the trees until late in the afternoon.

'He is leaving! He is leaving!'

The words seemed to repeat and repeat themselves in her mind.

She had a bath, then stood staring at

her wardrobe to wonder, woman-like, what she would wear for the last time he would see her.

She was surprised that he had not asked to talk to her alone and she thought it was because her father had so much to say to him.

She felt sure, however, that if he wished to be with her he would make some excuse later in the evening.

Her thoughts returned again to her clothes.

Finally she chose a gown that she had not worn before, but had kept it for some important occasion which had never arisen.

It was white, like so many of her gowns, and of a soft chiffon which clung to her figure and made her look very sylph-like and at the same time very young.

Because she had washed her hair it seemed as if the sunbeams had been caught in it, and yet when she looked at herself before she left her bedroom she wished rather that she had the beauty of the goddess of the moon, which would please Lord Yelverton.

She thought perhaps when he was in Yukatan he would look up at the sky and think of her.

He would be alone and she also alone would be looking at the same moon hundreds of miles away.

'Shall I go with him?'

The question was there in her mind.

Then she knew she could not bear to be in the same category as the women who lived with her father for a short time and when they bored him were discarded as easily as yesterday's newspaper.

'It would spoil our love, it would take away the blessing of the Morning Star.'

What they had felt together in the spray from the cascade was sacred, and to her it was binding.

'I am his wife,' she said to herself, 'and because our union has been blessed I cannot and will not become his mistress!'

Her heart told her that she was being a fool and she was letting happiness slip from her grasp.

But her soul knew that her decision was right and she could not destroy her own ideals.

Slowly, although she wanted to hurry, she walked through the twisting passages to where she knew Lord Yelverton and her father would be waiting on the verandah.

They were there, and as she saw him dressed in his evening-clothes, her heart turned a somersault and she felt as if the world spun dizzily round her.

He smiled at her and she thought, although she was not sure, that there was a glint of admiration in his eyes.

Her father put out his hand and she took it thankfully as if she wanted to hold onto something.

'You are looking very lovely this evening, my dear,' he said. 'I ought to paint you in that gown.'

It was an effort, but Tula managed to laugh lightly.

'I would not look as decorative as Carlotta.'

'I am not sure,' he said. 'Now I look at you I think I have failed to realize that there was no need for me to employ a model from outside the house.'

'You are flattering me, Papa!' Tula said. 'And you know I should be a very restless model and you would be angry with me.'

She kissed his cheek and sat down in a chair near to him, aware all the time, although she did not look at him, that Lord Yelverton was watching her.

Then the children came rushing out from the house as if they were ravenously hungry, yet because Liza had tidied them they appeared cleaner and neater than usual.

Liza was carrying Petronella in her arms and she walked across to Ajax Audenshaw to say:

'Your youngest daughter wishes to say goodnight to you. She is almost asleep, but she insisted on coming to see you.'

Ajax Audenshaw rose and took Petronella in his arms.

She was an attractive child and she snuggled against him.

He looked down at her with an expression of affection on his face that made him look even more handsome than he usually did.

Tula glanced at Liza and knew that she was thinking the same as she was, except that the expression in her eyes told Tula what she had always suspected, that Liza loved her father.

'Perhaps one day,' she thought, 'Papa will realize he would be much happier with Liza than with those tiresome women who demand his attention and are interested in nothing but themselves.'

Petronella was almost asleep and Ajax Audenshaw bent and kissed her, then handed her back to Liza.

'She seems to be much better in health,' he remarked.

'She is perfectly well and happy since I have altered her diet,' Liza replied. 'She now sleeps well and is no longer fretful.'

'You are a clever woman!'

'I try to be,' she answered, 'because I love your children.'

'And not surprisingly they love you,' he replied.

She smiled and it made her look very attractive.

Tula found herself praying that what she hoped for would come true. Liza and her father could be a perfect combination.

Then there was a question in her mind.

If Liza were there permanently to see to him and the children, what would she do?

Instinctively she looked at Lord Yelverton.

She met his eyes and because she was afraid there would be a pleading expression in hers she hastily looked away again.

Fortunately dinner was announced at

that moment and they all went in, the children noisily rushing to their seats, watching expectantly for the first course.

Dolores arrived, which caused a commotion as the men had to rise to their feet and the boys did so reluctantly after an audible command from Liza.

'Do we have to dine at such an inconvenient hour?' Dolores enquired. 'The Spanish eat late, very late, at nine or ten o'clock. It is much more civilized.'

'Here we are either English or Mexican. Take your choice!' Ajax Audenshaw answered.

There was a note in his voice which made Tula glance at him sharply.

'He is growing bored with her,' she told herself, and was glad.

As far as she was concerned, Dolores had been the most unattractive of the women her father had brought to live with him.

She was sure that Dolores would not be dismissed without scenes and quarrels, recriminations and doubtless an exhibition of temper.

Tula knew how wearing this would be, for as usual she would have to bear much of the brunt of such a situation.

Then as if she sensed what might happen Dolores contrived with every allurement in her repertoire to hold Audenshaw's attention all through the meal.

When it was finished she drew him to one side as if she was determined to have him to herself.

The children rushed out into the garden and Tula found herself standing beside Lord Yelverton on the verandah.

'I have something to say to you,' he said in a low voice.

'What is it?' she enquired.

She had the feeling that he was going to ask her point-blank whether she was coming away with him or not.

Although she knew the answer, it would be hard to say and even harder to let him go.

She felt her whole body go tense and her fingers clenched until the nails dug into her palms.

'I lost something of great importance at the cascade,' Lord Yelverton said.

He spoke in a low voice as if he was afraid they might be overheard.

It was not what Tula had expected him to say and as she looked at him in surprise, he went on:

'I know it is late, but I need you to guide me there, as I am not certain of the way.'

'But, of course,' Tula agreed.

She knew why he was in a hurry, so that whatever he had lost could be packed to travel with him the next morning.

She had a feeling he was relieved at her agreement, but he merely said:

'Let us go at once. I have ordered the horses.'

'Shall I change?'

'There is no time for that. Come as you are.'

She was about to say that her gown was not wide enough for her to ride astride, but he took her by the arm and at his touch she felt everything fly out of her head.

All she knew was the thrill his hand gave her, and a sudden weakness which made it impossible not to acquiesce in anything he asked.

He drew her round the outside of the house and there she saw two horses waiting, and on one of them was a saddle with a pommel.

She smiled, thinking that the reason he had insisted she should go as she was was because he disliked her riding astride in her fringed skirt.

Lord Yelverton wasted no time.

He lifted her up into the saddle, arranged her skirt, then mounted his own horse without saying a word.

As she knew he expected, Tula rode ahead thinking as she did so, that they would take the quickest route to the cascade and should be there before it grew dark.

She wondered what he could have lost and was half-afraid to ask in case it was one of the precious treasures that had been in the cave.

Then she told herself that he need not worry even if it had been left behind.

No-one from the village was likely to go to the cascade at night, and she was sure that even in the day-time the peasants would be too superstitious because Diaz had been staying there, to touch anything that belonged to him.

As a Priest of Quetzalcoatl he too was sacred and they needed his blessing on their families and their crops.

The sun was just beginning to sink in a blaze of glory which was reflected in the sea and on the stream as soon as they were in sight of it.

The narrow paths Tula took made it impossible for her and Lord Yelverton to ride side by side.

But she was vividly conscious of him behind her and she wondered if he was thinking of tomorrow with excitement and perhaps with a little regret because he was leaving her behind.

'There will be new things for him to do, new treasures for him to discover, new people for him to meet,' she told herself, 'and I shall be forgotten.'

Once again it swept over her almost like a tidal wave that she was crazy to let him go alone.

Fate with inscrutable magic had brought them together, when by all the laws of Chance there had been no possibility of their meeting in this life, or in any other.

But they had met, and through a strange quirk of fate they had been married and blessed by the Morning Star.

'For him it was not enough,' Tula thought.

She wanted to cry out at the sheer agony she felt at being unable to have the man she loved.

'He wants me, but that is not enough. He wants me as a woman as Papa wants Dolores, and all those other women.'

She thought that to men like her father and Lord Yelverton women were like flowers, beautiful and desirable until they were picked. Then they faded and not even their fragrance was left behind.

They climbed slowly, and now the narrow sheeptrack began to descend into the valley.

A few minutes later Tula could hear the familiar murmur of the cascade, at first little more than the buzz of a bee, then growing louder.

Now it was the music that had been the background for her thoughts, her feelings and her love all the time she had been nursing Lord Yelverton.

She had a strange feeling as if they were coming home together; a man and wife returning to where they belonged and where their happiness lay.

'Perhaps when we get there,' Tula

thought, 'he will kiss me goodbye. Then, although I will hear him go, I will not watch him ride away tomorrow morning.'

She told herself that would be best for them both, and out of sight she would be able to control her tears.

The sound of the cascade grew louder, and now as they rounded the rock Tula could see directly below her the place where they had slept in their tents.

Then to her astonishment she saw that the tents were still there.

She remembered that Lord Yelverton had said—or was it she who had suggested? —that his servants could collect them.

They had obviously forgotten to do so, and now it would delay his departure in the morning, although she was not certain if that made her glad or sorry.

She could not believe that what he had left behind was merely the tents, for if he had remembered they were still there he could have sent his servants, while they were having dinner, to bring them back.

There would have been plenty of time for them to do so in the daylight.

Tula's horse reached the flat green ground where they had camped and she slipped from the saddle.

She left her horse and walked towards the stream, aware as she did so that Lord Yelverton who had been a little behind her had also dismounted.

When he had done so, he took the bridle from his horse's head and placed it on the ground. Then he removed the bridle from Tula's horse.

It surprised her, although she knew it meant the horses would be able to crop the short grass more easily.

It also pleased her because she thought he was obviously in no hurry to get back and wished to talk to her.

'At least we shall not be disturbed,' she thought.

Then she was afraid of what they had to say to each other.

Supposing he tried to persuade her to

go with him and refused to take 'no' for an answer.

She knew it was something she did not want to argue about.

It would be an embarrassment to both of them and might spoil their memories of each other when they were parted.

'I must try to make him understand,' Tula said to herself.

At the same time, she was not only afraid of what he might say, but of what she herself, would feel.

'I want him! I want him desperately!' she thought, and felt herself tremble as he joined her beside the stream.

'I am afraid your servants forget to collect your tents,' she said.

'I did not tell them to take them away.'

'You forgot? I should have reminded you, but I have not seen you all day.'

'Yes, I know,' he said, 'it is not easy in your house to have a quiet conversation with anyone.'

Tula smiled.

'I was just thinking we would not be interrupted here.'

'I am glad of that.'

There was silence and because it made Tula feel a little shy she said: 'What have you lost? We must look for it.'

'I have lost something very important,' Lord Yelverton replied, 'and I have brought you here because you are the only person who can find it for me.'

'Of course I will find it, if it is possible,' Tula said. 'What am I to look for?'

Again there was silence, and she thought he came a little nearer to her.

'I have lost my heart, Tula!'

It was not the answer she had expected, and because it frightened her she put up her hands as if to defend herself.

'N...no...please...do not say...that,' she pleaded. 'I thought you...understood...I thought you realized when I did not...come and find you today that I...cannot do what you want.'

'How do you know what I want?' Lord

Yelverton enquired.

'You told me...last night.'

'I think what I said last night misled you, as I have been misled.'

She did not understand and she looked at him puzzled, conscious as she did so, how attractive he looked.

The sun had left the valley and now it was only touching the top of the cascade and turning it to gold.

Tula could see him silhouetted against it and it seemed to her he was an Aztec warrior with a helmet of gold above his flowing robe.

'I think really,' Lord Yelverton said in a quiet voice, 'there is no need for any explanations between us, and why I have brought you here tonight, Tula, is so that we can start our honeymoon without fear of interruption, alone together as we have been in our minds, and perhaps our spirits since you saved my life.'

The way he spoke made Tula tremble,

but still she did not understand.

'H...honeymoon?' she faltered.

She thought sadly that she could not stay as he wished her to do and she must hurt him when she rode away.

'We are married!' Lord Yelverton said. 'Have you forgotten?'

'I shall never forget,' she replied, 'but it was not the...same for you.'

'Only I can say if that is true or not,' he answered.

She did not reply, and after a moment he went on:

'Tell me, Tula, if I left you tomorrow, as I think you expect me to do, would you, if you never saw me again, believe that our marriage in the spray made me your husband for all time?'

Because she thought her answer was not what he wanted to hear Tula could not look at him, and there was a long pause before she said in a voice that was little above a whisper:

'Y...yes.'

'That is what I thought,' Lord Yelverton said, 'and yet you were prepared to send me away and remain unmarried for the rest of your life.'

'It...may seem very strange to you...and perhaps very...stupid,' Tula said, 'but I knew when we were blessed by the Morning Star that no other man could mean anything in my life.'

'No man ever will!' Lord Yelverton said firmly.

He drew nearer still and put out his arms.

'Please... Please...listen to me!' Tula begged. 'Because I feel like...this and because I know that for you it was different...you must...go away... There is no need to worry about me. I shall have...many things to do...and I am deeply grateful because you have given me such...happiness.'

'Will that be enough?' Lord Yelverton asked, 'for you, or for me?'

'It...has to be!'

She was afraid she might disappoint him and said quickly:

'I do not want to...hurt you, but because it would be wrong and spoil our love...I cannot go with you.'

'I think too,' Lord Yelverton said in his deep voice, 'that you feel you could not lower yourself to be like those women with whom your father tried to forget your mother.'

Once again, Tula thought, he was reading her thoughts, and because it was impossible to speak she merely nodded her head.

'Last night before I kissed you,' Lord Yelverton went on, 'I was thinking only how interesting and exciting it would be to have you with me in Yukatan. Because we have lived in a strange enchanted and perhaps god-like world these last days, I had almost forgotten there are social conventions and dozens of other restrictions outside this place where we are now standing.'

He paused, then put his arms around her as he said:

'After I kissed you, I came to my senses.'

He felt her quiver as he touched her. Then as if it was impossible to fight him she turned and hid her face against his shoulder.

'What I realized was that I was no longer a single person thinking only of myself,' Lord Yelverton said very gently, 'but that I am now a part of you, as you are a part of me. It would be impossible for me to go through my life without you.'

He knew that Tula took a deep breath and he said:

'We are therefore, my darling, married not only by Quetzalcoatl, important though he may be, but also according to the laws of Mexico!'

Tula gave a little cry and raised her head to look at him.

'What are you...saying to...me?'

'I am telling you that because I felt

it would be a farce for you and me to go through a Church marriage after our wedding in the spray, I have married you this afternoon in the Civil Court of Acapulco!'

Because she was so astonished Tula could only stare at him, and he said with a smile:

'It was not as difficult as it sounds. For foreigners all that was required was the written consent of your father, and your Birth Certificate. Fortunately I had mine with me.'

'We are...married?'

It was difficult for Tula to breathe the words.

'We are legally married,' Lord Yelverton answered, 'but I think, my precious, that the only marriage that will matter to either of us is the one that took place in the spray.'

'Do you mean that? Do you really...mean it?'

'I swear to you I mean it,' he answered,

'but I was not certain how much it meant and how deeply it affected me until I kissed you and you told me that you loved me.'

The way he spoke made her feel shy and Tula buried her head once again on his shoulder, as he said:

'Not in words, but when I touched you we became indivisible, and you were in my heart as the breath of life you gave me is in my body.'

Tula made a little incoherent exclamation. Then he realized she was crying.

'My darling, my sweet,' he said, 'what have I said to make you unhappy?'

'It...it is because I am...so happy,' she whispered through her tears. 'I...I thought today I had lost you...you would...leave me at dawn and I would never see...you again!'

'You will not only see me,' Lord Yelverton replied, 'but you will be with me for the rest of our lives, and perhaps in the eternity which exists beyond that.'

Tula raised her head, and although he saw that her cheeks were wet, her eyes were shining.

'I love you! I...love you!' she cried. 'How can I make you...realize how much I...love you?'

'There will be plenty of time for us to tell each other of our love,' Lord Yelverton said, 'and because I want this night to be a very special one for you, as well as for me, my darling, I want you to put on now the gown in which you were married in the spray.'

'I would...like to do...that.'

'I am sure it is there in your tent,' Lord Yelverton said.

He released her from his arms as he spoke, and he thought as he looked at her in the last light of the sun he had never seen any woman look so radiant!

The tears were still on her cheeks, like the spray from the cascade, her radiance was like the sun touching the top of it and giving it a halo of gold.

Tula stood for one moment looking at him. Then as if she wanted to obey him she ran towards her own tent and Lord Yelverton went to his.

As he expected the white Mexican trousers he had worn for their wedding were where he had left them and he put them on, leaving his chest bare as it had been on Diaz's instructions.

It did not take him long but when he went outside the sun had vanished and the first stars were beginning to appear in the translucence of the sky.

He looked up at them, then sensing rather than hearing her he knew Tula was there.

She was walking towards him through the shadows, her gown with its Indian embroidery round the hem, gleaming white against the greenery and she had released her hair over her bare shoulders.

He thought it would be impossible for any woman to look more lovely and at the same time so pure and spiritual as if in fact, she was a goddess come down to earth.

He did not move, but waited for her to join him and only then did he put his arms around her and hold her close.

'Do you know how beautiful you are?'

'Tell me...please, darling...tell me! I have been so afraid you do not admire me and I am not...good enough for you.'

'How can one not admire the moon, the stars, or the flowers?' he asked. 'You are all these things and so much more.'

She pressed herself closer.

'I love you! It is all I can think of to say...and because I love you there is...nothing else in the...world except...you.'

His lips were on her forehead and she thought what in their Marriage Service he had said as he kissed her brow.

As if once again her thoughts were easy for him to read he said:

'I kiss your brow, my darling, as you kissed my feet. In a little while I am going to kiss you all over your perfect body, and especially your feet because I worship you!'

'You must not...say such things,' Tula whispered. 'I am not...worthy, but I knew when I kissed your feet that I was ready to follow you bare-foot...across the world if you only...loved me as I love...you.'

'I love you!' Lord Yelverton said, 'and I have nothing of importance to give you except myself and my love.'

'That is all I want,' she murmured, 'but will my love be enough?'

He smiled.

'I think we have so much in common, my darling, that it will take us a lifetime to discover everything that each of us needs. So even apart from our love, we will be enthralled, intrigued and excited by each other.'

Tula gave an exclamation of sheer happiness and put her head against his shoulder, then she realized he was naked and he knew she blushed.

He laughed very gently.

'My darling,' he said, 'I am prepared for you to teach me about the gods, but I have many human things to teach you and it will be the most exciting thing I have ever done in my life.'

'I...want to learn,' Tula said, 'and you must teach me about love...so that I will not...disappoint you.'

'You will never do that. You are like a cave which contains so many marvellous and precious things that we can only anticipate the wonder of what we shall find.'

'I shall pray and pray that you will go on discovering new things about me, so that you will never want to go...excavating in...love, anywhere...else.'

Lord Yelverton laughed.

'You can be quite sure of that. You will delight and enthral me, and I suspect even surprise and puzzle me so that the treasure you give me is endless and inexhaustible.'

'I hope so,' Tula said. 'I hope I shall always seem like that to you, but please...you will have to help me.'

'Do you think I wish to do anything else?' Lord Yelverton asked. 'And, my precious, you know that I belong to you, just as you belong to me. You gave me the kiss of life, and I am living at this very moment in this particular place where I should have died but for you.'

His arms tightened around her and he said, close to her lips:

'I am very glad I am alive, and also very excited.'

She lifted her mouth to his and then he was kissing her, kissing her wildly, passionately, demandingly with kisses which she knew drew them closer and closer to each other until as she felt his heart beating against hers, she knew it would be impossible for time or man ever to separate them.

As Lord Yelverton kissed her the darkness fell and the stars came out overhead brilliant and sparkling in the sable of the sky while the moon rose slowly over the trees and touched the cascade with silver.

Still they stood locked together with a closeness that seemed part of the music of the water.

Then Tula felt Lord Yelverton's fingers undoing the string that fastened her gown.

When he did so it fell softly to the ground like the ghost of a sigh.

He took his arms from her and stood back for a moment to look at her silver, white, exquisite as a Greek statue in the moonlight.

He knew that she filled the shrine in his heart that had always been empty and that she was everything he had always looked for in a woman and thought it impossible ever to find.

Because she was aroused to an ecstasy that was divine she was not shy in her nakedness but stood looking at him with eyes that seemed to fill her face, and yet there was the faint reflection of the stars in them.

She thought for one moment that he would kneel and kiss her feet, then his need of her made him instead pick her up in his arms.

'I love you, my darling!' he said. 'I love and worship you, but I also want you!'

She gave a little cry of happiness as he carried her away into the shadows and secrecy of his tent...

This Large Print Book for the Partially sighted, who cannot read normal print, is published under the auspices of

THE ULVERSCROFT FOUNDATION